I. K. (Isaac Kahn) Friedman, Isaac Kahn Friedman

The Lucky Number

I. K. (Isaac Kahn) Friedman, Isaac Kahn Friedman

The Lucky Number

ISBN/EAN: 9783743388895

Manufactured in Europe, USA, Canada, Australia, Japa

Cover: Foto ©Andreas Hilbeck / pixelio.de

Manufactured and distributed by brebook publishing software (www.brebook.com)

I. K. (Isaac Kahn) Friedman, Isaac Kahn Friedman

The Lucky Number

THE LUCKY NUMBER

BY

I. K. FRIEDMAN

CHICAGO

WAY AND WILLIAMS

1896

CONTENTS

Chauvinism at Devereux's

"Patriotism is the last refuge of a scoundrel."
—DR. JOHNSON.

DEVEREUX is a Frenchman — his name has told you that at a glance; he is a Frenchman out of France, a fish out of water, and the water is cleaner for the absence of the fish. Anxious as France is for an increased population she offered every inducement in the world to Devereux, and those of his compatriots who frequent his saloon, to stay in America. They had left their country to our country's detriment, true patriots they.

L'Auberge, so Devereux named his place, and The Lucky Number (a saloon one block removed from L'Auberge in distance, a mile in caste) represent the two extreme points on the crooked line of vice : L'Auberge

7

symbolizes the attractiveness of crime, The Lucky Number its repulsiveness; the one tempts men to sin, the other punishes them when they fall; a career of evil starts in a place like Devereux's and ends in a place like The Lucky Number;—so much for the spirit of these dives, just a word or two about the letter.

At Devereux's you may look down on a polished oak floor and up at a richly ornamented ceiling; you may draw a cane-bottom chair, neatly varnished, up to a cherry-stained table, sip your absinthe out of a thin, shining glass, and see just how you look as you do it in the beveled mirror which covers the wall back of the mahogany bar. If your taste run toward art, you may indulge it by admiring the copies in oil of Bougereau's paintings—*honi soit qui mal y pense.*

The Lucky Number is a crude study in dirt, done in rough pine; in some places this dirt is thicker than in others, and thus the monotone is relieved,—beyond this there is no attempt made at the decorative. If you look down you will see sawdust and dust; if you look up, look out for your head.

The *clientèle* at Devereux's is composed of two distinct types; the one is best described by the French term *sâle-type*, a term I prefer to leave untranslated; the other is made up of "fine workers," forgers, counterfeiters and thieves, who represent the intellect of vice, and draw the plans and lay the plots for the muscle, the labor, of vice to carry out. They have a way, all their own, of covering and retracing their tracks, which baffles and discourages the most persistent of sleuths. Yet detection is easy as compared with arrest, for the rascals never seem to get farther than the station steps; there they always pause, lift their hats in the most approved Parisian style, bid the officers a *bon soir*, and disappear. It is impossible not to admire their manners.

Safe in jail,—when the police get them that far you may be sure they are safe,—then the work has but begun, for to convict them is quite another matter. They play a game of wit, a game of which they are past-masters, and one worth winning only when they hold the bad cards. Let an illustration serve.

A complicated plot, finished in every detail, was laid for the murder of a miser; this miser, moreover, was a Frenchman, and lived in a hovel in the French quarter—two things which made the job hazardous, nay, foolhardy; because they would certainly be suspected of the crime an hour after its execution. To let suspicion fall elsewhere and fall there naturally, not to jerk it there—here is where the finesse, the adroitness of the plot centered. The combined astuteness of their depraved minds, fitted by long training for such work, was taxed to solve the difficult problem; but the solution was as nice, as logical and as perfect as a definition in calculus. One fault only could be found, it was too nice; let the smallest cog slip by so much as a hair's breadth, and the ponderous machine would hurl them to death in the balance wheel.

This they knew, and their knowledge made them shudder, and their shuddering made them consider and reconsider; finally they gave it up; but it was fascinating, and the fascination was made more intense by the condition of their purses.   They had had a hard winter, *"un hiver moral,"* to use the expression of one of them.   Blood was one thing, money another, and they meant to have that miser's money, *coûte que coûte*, cost what it might.

But that one cog slipped—it always does somehow,—and the result was not so disastrous as expected; they were too familiar with machinery of that kind not to be prepared for accidents.   Its every movement had been calculated to a fraction, and by a fraction four of them escaped its iron jaws.   The fifth, as accomplished in mathematics as the rest but slower in movement, was caught by the foot and pulled out by the police.

The evidence of these four was needed to convict the fifth, and the police and the press started in hot pursuit; but the four could not be found; where they went was a mystery, but mystery or no, they were gone —they had taken French leave, as it were.

The state's attorney was on his metal, for this was his first important case, and he wanted to show the public of what stuff he was made. He was ambitious, too, this state's attorney; his eye had long been fixed upon a seat on the Supreme bench, and if he missed this chance he was likely to remain standing where he now was. He let the police go their way and the press go its way, he pursued the even tenor of his own.

He took the tangled skein of facts and clues in his prehensile hands, and unravelled it carefully, bit by bit; in the mass of this untangled stuff he discovered one little thread which repaid him for his hard labor and staying awake o' nights. By that thread he gained this nugget of information; a certain Godier knew the whereabouts of the foxy four (such was the euphonious title now bestowed upon them), and kept his accomplices informed of every important move made by their arch-enemies. This was the part Godier was to play by prearrangement —these great generals of crime calculated on victory, but they made the necessary preparations for a possible defeat. Now the thing was to catch this Godier and make him speak.

He was located at Devereux's without the least difficulty. The detective who captured him said, ''The job was as easy as picking a penny from the street;'' but to make him speak, that was like lifting a house from its foundation.

The man acted the deaf mute, and he acted like one created for the part by nature. After much trouble and casting about some one was found who could speak French and read the deaf and dumb alphabet, but that some one could not understand Godier, who spoke a *digital patois*.

They put him in the sweat-box and turned the steam on at full force, but never a word could they sweat out of him. Then they tried to flatter him to speech by the liberal application of a club, but his tongue did not prove susceptible to flattery. He gesticulated violently, he writhed and turned with the agility of a contortionist, but he would not speak; he ground his set teeth, he became blue in the face, he buried his long finger nails in the flesh of his palms, his throat seemed bursting in a convulsive effort at speech, but not even a monosyllable did he utter.   The expression on his countenance, the pathetic appeal of his dumb lips, the muscular contraction of his throat made the pantomime appalling.   If you have ever seen a mute trying to call for assistance when in danger, you can form an idea of how Godier conducted himself through the ordeal.

The state's attorney sickened at the cruel performance and he ordered it to be stopped. He began to question the possibility, not to say probability, of a mere sham withstanding the fierce rays of such a powerful searchlight without discovering his mask.   Yet to believe the rascal's dumbness other than a feint was to acknowledge the hopelessness of the case.   That seat on the Supreme bench seemed farther away than in the distant day of his dreamy youth.   With hands crossed behind his back, he paced up and down his office restlessly, and urged his brain with whip and lash. In the throes of intellectuality his thought gave birth to an idea—ah, there was an easier and less painful way of bringing this mute to speech!

He released Godier, and sent for a detective by the name of Gilchrist. Gilchrist, a Canadian of French descent, had this in his favor: he spoke French fluently, and he was tenacious. "I am a tenacious bird, I am," were the words constantly on his lips. Tenacity was the one quality the state's attorney pinned his faith to, and this is why he sent for Gilchrist. Aside from the undue development of this one trait, he was an ordinary mortal endowed with but little more than ordinary acumen; he was not one of those superhuman detectives, existing only in the minds of fictionists, who start with a speck of dust and end with the creation of a cosmos.

When released, Godier made straight for L'Auberge; at first blush this may seem madness, but reflect a little and you will see method. When he entered, Gilchrist, who had preceded him, was reading *Le Carica-*

ture with an apparently absorbing interest. "There's the mute," the detective heard some one behind him say in a low voice, and this was the only comment passed on Godier's sudden acquittal; it was evidently taken as a matter of course.   The detective watched (well, do you know how detectives watch? They watch as a cat watches a mouse), but he never saw so much as a surreptitious glance pass between the mute and his boon companions.   The tongue-tied wretch seated himself at the nearest table, put his doubled fist to his mouth and tossed back his head; Devereux understood what all this meant, for he placed a pint of claret and a glass on the table, and the mute nodded approval.

Gilchrist, like the state's attorney, was now besieged by doubt; he did not know at first whether to believe the man a mute, or not to believe it.   A second afterwards he chided himself for being such a credulous fool.   Here he was just launching himself on an expedition for discovery, and doubting the existence of the object of his quest.   He needed no other spur than his own scolding to stir him to action; he arose and planted himself in front of his prey, leaned over and whispered in good French, "I have an important message from the four." The mute looked up with an expression of dumb amazement, the others tried to hide their laughter in their sleeves; one of them, a fellow of some wit, remarked, "He doesn't speak—French, sir." The detective tried hard not to appear disconcerted, lounged around a while and left. "Laugh at him, did they? he would show them before long that the last laugh is the merriest."

For the next two days he shadowed the place without entering; he was waiting outside for an inspiration, and when the inspiration came he was going inside, and that "jailbird" should speak or he would pull his tongue out by the roots.

Meanwhile, the state's attorney was suffering from nervous depression, brought on by the fear that his crown would be one of ridicule instead of glory. He summoned Gilchrist and lectured him. Three whole days had passed, and he had not discovered anything worthy of even reporting at head-quarters. How did he spend his time, sleeping? If he didn't wake up, and wake up with a start, he would have him discharged then and there. He gradually assumed a pleasant tone, promising to use his influence for the sleuth's promotion, if he but made Godier speak. "For once," he finished, with a quiet smile, "speech is golden, and silence is silver; remember it."

Humiliated by the lecture, but animated by the prize, Gilchrist walked out of the office, meekly muttering, "I am a tenacious bird, I am,"—which was his way of praying for inspiration, for the quality of tenacity, he thought, must appeal to the Lord, when all else failed. The inspiration came, and it came, as inspirations will, at the most unexpected time and in the most unexpected manner, just when his heart grew sick from hope deferred.

He fretted and fumed two more valuable days away shadowing Devereux's, and he was about as tired, disgusted and blue as it is possible for any mortal to be. This hanging around for an inspiration was a poor business and, tenacious as he was, he had had enough of it—Gilchrist wanted more substance and less shadow.

He walked home, donned a disguise,—it goes without saying that he was an adept at disguises,—and made for L'Auberge. He had met with such a thing as luck in his career, and he trusted to meet it again that night at Devereux's.

He was striding thither in the darkness, when he bumped into a negro carrying a mongrel musical instrument on his back. The "tenacious bird" shoved him aside impatiently and hurried on.

"By God, I have it!" he said, running back far more quickly than he had moved forward.

"See here, 'dingy,' can you play this tune?" Gilchrist whistled a few bars of a well known air.

"'Deed I can, boss! I know de tune, but not de name," said the negro, starting to take the instrument from his back.

"Never mind that; let's see if you can whistle the tune."

He whistled it better than Gilchrist had done. The detective pressed a silver dollar in this wandering minstrel's hand; he could be generous when occasion demanded.

"Do you know where Devereux's place is?"

"Where all dem Frenchies is? down there between——"

"Exactly, go there and play. Play anything you have a mind to play, but don't start that tune until I come, and when I come don't play it until I step on your foot. You understand, not until I step on your foot. One word more, you don't know me, and you never saw me before."

He held another dollar to the light, "If you do the right thing, this is yours; go ahead, and I'll follow."

The negro's instrument has been called mongrel because I know of no better adjective to describe the contrivance. It was a combination of everything that makes accordant sound, and discordant, too, for that matter; cymbal and harp, trumpet and mouth-organ, and drum and fife—all were included. The simultaneous use of feet, hands and mouth was required, and one needed to be a born musician as well as a born gymnast to play it.

The minstrel almost knocked Gilchrist's best laid plans into a cocked hat by starting his performance at L'Auberge with "Die Wacht Am Rhein;" luckily he saw his mistake, made evident by hisses and groans, and he substituted "Yankee Doodle," followed by "Hail Columbia;" this the patrons liked better and they applauded.

At this point Gilchrist stepped in—he appeared excited and out of breath. Had they heard the news? War had been declared in France! Guns had been fired! Troops were mobilized! The navy was on the move! German soldiers had marched into Madagascar! He had just seen the announcement on a special bulletin in the *Tribune* office.

They jumped from their seats and crowded near him. He glanced around; Godier was there with the rest; so far so good.

"I must hasten," he said, "before dawn every Frenchman in the city must know it." Then came a torrent of wherefores and whys and whens.

The detective knew that the characteristic of the Gallic mind is to excite itself first and to reason afterwards, and he answered accordingly, but his answers were consistent; they came as swiftly as their queries and more swiftly, but thus far not a question from Godier; did he smell a rat?

The news spread; men, women and children came rushing in from all directions; the place became so crowded that one could hardly turn. Gilchrist never had known that there were so many French out of France. A throng gathered outside, and Devereux shut the doors, begging them to make less noise, saying, "The police will shut me up for a public nuisance, if you keep on yelling."

Gilchrist started to go. "There was much to be done, there were other places besides this." They held him by the coat, "Just a word, just one word more."

"Well, he would remain long enough to drink to France and to victory." He laid a crisp bill on the bar. "A drink for every one out of that;" who would be stingy on such an occasion? He filled the glasses and cried, *"Vive la France! Vive la France! à bas les Allemands!"* They took up the cry in unison; you could have heard it blocks and blocks away. This enthusiasm warmed their blood and made them recklessly generous; then the corks began to fly. It was a banner day for Devereux—nothing like war for his business. The more they drank the louder they yelled, and the louder they yelled the more they drank.

And Godier? He was the one silent individual in the place, was Godier, but he understood and heard—Gilchrist could tell that from his ears.

Now or never. The "tenacious bird" touched the negro's foot and the Marseillaise began with a vim; the musician was playing for a dollar, and he wanted to give a dollar's worth. The angel Gabriel appearing there in person and blowing the Marseillaise on his celestial trumpet could not have evoked more wonder and surprise, so suddenly and so unexpectedly did the music burst forth.

Gilchrist made the best of a rare opportunity, and shouted rather than sang the opening strophe of the battle hymn:

"Ye sons of freedom, wake to glory,
    Hark! hark! what myriads bid you rise!
Your children, wives, and grandsires hoary,
    Behold their tears, and hear their cries!"

The first was all he sang unaccompanied, then the others took it up, and how they took it up. They threw their arms around each other and whirled about in patriotic ecstasy; they sang and shouted and screamed with all their might and all their main. Chairs and tables were smashed beyond the hope of repair, and Devereux did not even cry halt; he urged them on by his own example. When it came to the chorus:

"To arms! to arms! ye brave!
    The avenging sword unsheathe;
March on! march on
To victory or death!
To victory or death!"—

he fired glass after glass on the floor from behind the bar. Old Planard, "the lame devil," who had lost a leg in the last war and was proud of it, kept time with his wooden stump; the dull thud of that stump was the one sound discernible in the uproar.

Exiles, castaways, most of them, they were pouring all their woes, all their hatred, all their regrets, all their homesickness, all that was bad and all that was good in them, into the stirring verses of the Marseillaise; every word was a key which opened the shut chambers of their hearts to long, long vistas of a happier past. Women were sobbing hysterically, and children were clinging to their mothers in fright; but the battle-hymn went on and on, and gathered force as it went.

The negro was carried away by the spirit of the others, and he made that mongrel instrument do the work of a band, and do it well. The sweat rolled down his face, the veins on the top of his bald head swelled to a violet blue; it seemed that his cheeks would crack from the blowing, and that his eyes would fall from their sockets.

The Marseillaise had aroused their fathers to deeds of heroism; it was the song of the Revolution, it was the song of France, it was the battle-hymn of the Republic; thousands and thousands had died with those precious words on their lips, and thousands and tens of thousands had marched with everlasting glory to the strains of that thrilling melody. And they — they would sing until their hearts sank from exhaustion, and their voices ceased forever.

What a pandemonium it was! But there was all the sublimity of a storm, all the grandeur which follows in the wake of lightning and thunder, when the heavens open and send their heavy artillery plunging down the vast skies.

The *Ausgelassenheit*—the *abandon*,—how it ravished, how it intoxicated, how it entranced! No man could resist the magnetism, the spell of such a divine madness. Godier, the cautious, the crafty, the circumspect Godier, was swept away by patriotic fervor, and when they reached the flaming appeal of the lines:

"And lo! our fields and cities blaze,
    And shall we basely view the ruin,
While lawless force, with guilty stride,
    Spreads desolation far and wide,
    With crime and blood its hands embuing.
    To arms! to arms! ye brave!"—

he joined in vociferously.

The detective knew not whether to laugh at him or cry for him; Gilchrist's French blood had been heated to the boiling point by the flames of this glowing fire of patriotism, and he was as thoroughly in earnest as the rest. Only by fooling himself had he fooled Godier; for the mute, suspecting a trap from the very first, had turned the strong damper of his will against the expanding heat of his emotions that threatened to tear him open unless he gave them vent; but when he saw Gilchrist singing with an enthusiasm too intense to be simulated,—and he was too shrewd an observer to be tricked by a spurious article,—his suspicions became disarmed, and he threw the safety-valve wide open and let the steam escape.

His lusty voice and vigorous lungs, like the arrival of fresh cohorts to fatigued troops, stimulated his countrymen, who were beginning to flag from sheer weariness, to greater efforts than had yet been achieved. The chandeliers shook, actually shook, and the very walls vibrated from the onslaught of the waves of sound.

The police, dressed in citizens' clothes, filed in one by one, but they were as little heeded as the poor flies which went buzzing about the room distractedly, and which had been shocked out of their hibernation by the clatter and din.

They were singing the chorus for the last time, and they gathered all their remaining force and vigor to make the words significant. They sang those verses as the rabble, marching towards Versailles in the stormy days of the revolution, must have sung them. This last chorus, if I may so phrase it, was a crescendo that progressed geometrically, a wave which gathered the multiplied force of every other wave that preceded it, and towered above them all mountain high.   You would have thought they were singing on the battle-fields amid the clashing of swords, the blowing of bugles, the screaming of shells and the roaring of cannon; nay, you would have heard the exultant shout of a victorious army drowning the agonizing cries of the defeated, the bleeding, the wounded and the dying.

Then they were silent, and the silence was as expressive as the song—you could have heard the quivering of an aspen leaf.

Gilchrist grasped Godier by the shoulder. Poor Godier! he felt his mistake intuitively. The police pressed forward and pushed the crowd back.

What a triumph for Gilchrist! For him it was the apotheosis of tenacity.   He would not have been a Frenchman had he not ended the third act of this drama with an epigram. "Gentlemen," said he, "the Marseillaise is the greatest general of France, under its leadership I have captured the enemy."

Rouge et Noir

HE held his last dime tightly in his closed fist, and elbowed his way to the dealer's table through the ragged crowd of vagabonds of all descriptions and occupations (save honest ones), who jostled and pushed to gain the coigns of vantage near the wheel. The place—filthy, bare, reeking with the smell of cheap whisky and still cheaper tobacco — was in perfect keeping with its patrons. The only things in the room, either ornamental or useful, were the gambling implements and the large kerosene lamp suspended from the ceiling, which gave forth a little, dim, flickering light and much foul odor.

He bet on the red, held his breath and shut his eyes, not daring to look; that dime symbolized a lodging for the night, and outside the blizzard was playing the deuce

with thinly clad, overcoatless wretches like
himself.

The wheel stopped with a loud clack—
red! He had won—the goddess of luck be
praised for that. He tucked this open
sesame to Black Tom's Cave of Comfort (a
basement lodging house, or better, a hcap of
bunks in a basement) way down in the
pocket of what was once a vest, and bet
again.

It was for a supper this time. A full supper, from soup to coffee, can be had for
eight cents by those who know where to go,
and who are contented with the quality of
the soup, the coffee, and what comes between
—the quantity is always satisfactory. No
food had crossed his lips all day, and the
issue between red and black made an empty
stomach palpitate with fear and excitement.

Red! and the supper was his, and he
smacked his lips with a pregustatory relish
—that coffee. For once in his ill-starred life
luck was favoring him, and he meant to
seize the opportunity. He doubled his
stakes,—the wheel stopped square at the red.

He tripled his stakes; bed, lodging, supper, cigar, whiskey (luxuries unknown to
him for months) and all! A whirl!—and the
wheel started again. He cursed himself
inwardly for being such a hazardous fool and
not knowing when to stop. If he had saved
only bed and supper, and had bet the rest!
Thrice around sped the circle glowing with
color. It stopped, wavered a second between the two, as if hesitating whether to
throw this dare-devil supperless into the
cold, or let him revel in luxury; then the red
had it. Eyes from all parts of the room shot
envious glances at him—eager, wolfish eyes,
aglow with want and hunger. Why couldn't
they have luck like that?

He grew reckless, the tide was flowing his
way, and on it he meant to ride to fortune;
he bet against all kinds of odds and still the
red, always the red. "He has charmed the
wheel," muttered some one.

The dealer had enough of this fool, fa-
vored by fortune as all fools are, and he
cried halt. The lucky gamester, envied but
reviled by the unlucky, made his way to the

door, jingling the silver in his pocket, and imagining all kinds of delightful tastes and sensations.

All this was the empty dream of a poor devil awakened from a restless sleep by the gnawing pains of hunger. A second or two passed before he could fully realize that it was all a dream, and he even smacked his lips once or twice like one who has eaten heartily of substantial food—so vividly had he seen these things in his mind's eye.

He sat upright and tried to think. A sudden bump on the head recalled him from the mimic world of dreams to the real world of facts and things. There he was exhausted from hunger, trying to sleep in one of the upper bunks in The Cave of Comfort. He lay flat on his back, pressed his hands to his stomach and moaned. If that dream were only true. He tried to sleep again, but the heavy snoring of the drunken or worn-out sleepers, who were piled around him on all sides like so much lumber, kept him awake. He was cold, too, and the basement air chilled him to the bone, de-

spite the heavy horse blanket, and the fact
that he had on every stitch of his clothing—
the only way to keep clothes in such a place.

The little wood stove in the corner threw
out all smoke and no heat, the atmosphere
(used to it as he was) choked him, and he
started to cough, when an ominous growl
from the bunk below warned him to keep his
cough to himself. By way of distraction he
fastened his sight on the flame of the small
lamp, burning low, which stood at the doorway near the seat of Black Tom, the Cer-
berus of this Hades. The longer he watched,
the brighter seemed the flame that circled
around the glass chimney like a red hoop of
living fire. Red again—it was the finger of
fortune beckoning him on.

Like a man moved by divine impetus, he
left all consequences out of reckoning and
clambered down. Black Tom, sitting half
asleep on his stool near the door, grumbled
a little, lifted his lamp from the floor, and
let him out. The man of fortune pulled
himself up the basement steps and found
himself in the deserted streets.

He had been in the cold but a minute and he was shaking from head to foot, his teeth chattering, and every limb trembling as if palsy-stricken. Thin veiling would have been about as much protection as those clothes of his, and then he had an empty stomach and a system wasted by hunger and exhaustion.

Too weak to move, he rested against a lamp-post, wondering what crazy notion had made him forsake a warm, comfortable bed (all things go by comparison) for that bleak, bitter cold street. Fortune, luck — those were things in which fools and capitalists should believe.

A clock from the tower of the neighboring depot struck ten clear, resonant strokes through the frosty air; he had believed the hour to be much later on account of the deserted appearance of the street; but in weather like this every rat that has a hole crawls into it for shelter. Ten o'clock—well, there might be hope yet.

Three jolly fellows, evidently the worse for an evening of intense gayety, staggered past.

The seeker of fortune tried to look more wretched than he was (difficult task) and begged for charity with a piteous tale. There was a slight patter of silver on the pavement, more welcome to the beggar's ears than a symphony from heaven. It was a dime! A strip of red, shaped like an inverted V, seemed to spurt from the sky to the ground.

The coin acted like a draught of new wine on his enervated system; fed by the promise of his dream he felt as if he had dined like a king, and through his stiff cramped body a current of fresh life began to run.

He moved cautiously but quickly down the dark alley like one afraid of some lurking danger, but yet familiar with his way. The gambling den of his dream was the object of his search, and for it he made straightway. Three short, quick raps, the slipping of a heavy bolt, and the door opened from within. The room, faces, positions, lights and shadows, perspective and all, seemed copied from the picture of his dream.

He pressed forward with a certain swagger of self-confidence and bet his dime on the red; not in the least disturbed by the dealer's sarcastic smile at the insignificant stake.

A whirr!—red and black coalesced and separated, separated and coalesced so quickly and so continually that no eye could follow. The wheel slowed down, oscillated a second or two, and then stopped. "And the black has it," sang out the dealer in a voice that plainly said "and I knew it." The dreamer of beautiful dreams, with fists firmly clenched, head bent down, and a curse on his lips, slunk back into the bleak street, his faith in dreams lost forever.

A Monger of Ballads

"I can make chansons, ballades, lais, virelais, roundels, and I am very fond of wine."
—A Lodging for the Night.

AN emaciated body covered with filthy rags; a repulsive face pinched and puckered by want and disease; half-shut lifeless eyes that peered cautiously from two deep-sunken sockets; a sensual red nose, that seemed to droop rather than curve over an unusually large mouth—such was Charcoal, the abstract and brief chronicle of the vice of the slums. Hated by thieves and thugs for the cowardice that made him a lackey for the lowest vagabonds, he represented something below zero on the social thermometer of the district.

Had you cast a single glance at him, as he sat busily writing at a table in one corner of The Lucky Number, you would have, understood why he was dubbed Charcoal by the birds of his own black feather.

He was evidently absorbed in what he was doing, so absorbed that he never stopped to sip from the huge schooner of beer that foamed temptingly at his elbow. There was little to disturb him, for it was the hour when honest people start to work; the slums were still wrapped in drunken sleep, the saloon was empty, and the scribe toiled on in comparative quiet and seclusion.

Finally he threw his stub of a pencil on the floor, leaned far back in his chair, gave a long yawn of satisfaction, and sipped his beer, as a god, "careless of mankind," reclines on the hills and sips nectar. The beer gone and the schooner turned upside down to discover a single drop lurking in the bottom, he took the greasy, brown paper in his still greasier fingers and examined his work with a critical cock of his crossed eyes. He seemed satisfied for he smiled,—if the facial gymnastic that drew one lip up towards the nose and the other down towards the chin, could be called a smile.

"Something funny?" asked Mike the bartender, who had been watching him closely from behind the bar. Mike was the only man in the district who ever spoke to Charcoal without punctuating his remarks with a kick or a curse; for Mike marvelled how a man unacquainted with soap and white shirts could master the occult science of writing—"where ignorance is bliss." Moreover, this same Michael had seen such writing converted into money (a thing that happens rarely, even in the slums), and the pecuniary consideration in no wise lessened his reverence.

"No-op," was the answer to the bartender's query, "it's something serious."

"I likes 'em humorous; now that er un of yourn, "Steve O'Donnel's Wake," was a corker;" then, as if to bear out his statement, he sang in a raucous voice, the chorus:

> "There was fighters, there was biters
> There was tough, old dynamiters
> At Steve O'Donnel's wake."

"Trash, miserable trash!" yelled the maker of ballads. "I wrote it for the amusement of ignorant wretches, and I'm ashamed of myself; I never want to hear it again!" and down came the clenched fist on the table.

Mike was so surprised at this unwonted outburst that he passed no remark on the schooner which fell on the floor, shattered to pieces.

"I can beat it easily, I can write something worthy of a man far better than I am. Listen!"

He rose to his feet, his dead eyes sparkling with the fire of life, his cheeks flushing perceptibly, his hands trembling with excitement, as he stood with chest out and shoulders back, the position of one who respects himself. The metamorphosis was complete; inspiration turned him, for the nonce, into something like a man.

"Can that be Charcoal?" thought Mike.

In a quivering, high-pitched voice he read his song; a pathetic ditty, gracefully told. It was the story of an old man who passed up and down the little street of a village, day in, day out, playing the same old tune on a crazy fiddle. The children mocked him,

older people called him crazy; but the old
man, never heeding them, played on, stub-
bornly refusing to tell what the spirit that
moved him was.   But one day their rude
treatment arousing his anger, he turned
suddenly and spoke:—

> "It's the tune that I played to my daughter,
>> It's the tune that my Nell loved best;
> I play and I seem to see her,
>> My Nell in her grave at rest."

They never troubled him after that, and he
went his way unmolested:—

> "And never his tune has varied,
>> Not once in many a year.
> It's the same old tune that he fiddles,
>> It's the same old tune that we hear."

You have seen a spring send water, pure
and undefiled, bubbling up through a mass
of decayed, slimy vegetation—this tramp
and his song present an analogy.

"Good," spake Mike, when the reader sat
down mopping his brow with a rag which
did duty for a handkerchief; "good; have
one on me."   And waiving the formality of
an acceptance, he filled a schooner to the
brim and placed it on the bar.

The poet paid no attention to this gen-
erosity, not established by precedent, and
sat lost in reverie, tapping the pine table
with his fingers to the tune of something
that beat in a corner of his brain.

"Does yer want me to bring it to yer on
a silver tray?" asked the mixer of drinks
sarcastically.

Charcoal crossed the floor covered with
sawdust, but to the surprise of Mike he
turned his back to the bar and sat himself at
the piano—a crazy old tin-pan affair, much
the worse for long abuse and hard pounding.

"Has yer turned timperance?" This second grand effort at sarcasm remained, like
the first, unanswered and unheeded. The
mind of the balladmonger was soaring
above all things of the earth, earthy, into
the divine realms of music. With his fore-
finger he picked out, one by one, the notes
of the tune he wanted for his song. The
inspiration was sudden and he wished to
impress the tune firmly on his mind, before
it was gone forever, past recall. The fact
that several keys gave no response when

struck did not in the least discourage him; a note, whistled from his pointed lips, a kind of natural piano, was substituted with evident satisfaction to the musician.

"If he ain't crazy!" Mike suppressed the conclusion in a hearty draught from the schooner intended for Charcoal, and to him he paid no further attention.

The man at the piano, with many shakes of the head and unnumbered fresh starts, kept pounding away diligently and continuously; at length each separate note, beginning with the first and ending with the last, arranged itself in harmony with every other, and the resultant melody seemed a near enough outward reproduction of the inner conception to content the artist. Charcoal was a Jack of all trades, good at two. He shut the piano with a bang, and whistled the air over half a dozen times to make sure that not a note had escaped his memory.

"Where to?" Mike ceased in his perfunctory cleaning for a minute and looked up inquiringly at his guest about to depart.

"Oh, I know a Dutchman down here who can write notes," and with this rather ambiguous answer he slouched into the street.

"I 'spose them things comes natural-like to some," said the bar-tender, explaining to a patron the origin of the new tune he had been whistling all day,—"just like, well, just like mixin' drinks comes to others."

I stated *en passant* that Charcoal was a Jack of all trades, differing from the other versatile Jacks in that he was good at two. Time was when he might have claimed a fair mastery of a third; in his better days (and you have read too much of this story not to guess that he must have seen better days) he had trod the stage; but whether he shone as a high tragedian or a low comedian, the records of the theatre do not say. Kid Kelly, rude biographer of the slums—who takes pains to learn a man's history, when he judges it to have been so black that the subject of his biography, rather than suffer its narration, would pay him hush money in the shape of future service,—is authority for the statement that Charcoal drew a big audience and a fat salary until he fell in love with a leading lady, fair as foul, who led him down the way to Avernus, made easy by the abuse of whiskey. As six out of every ten men (to make a rough guess) not born in the slums are sent there by whiskey or women, I am warranted by mathematical probability in accepting Kid's statements as truth, after deducting a certain percentage for exaggeration. Moreover, Charcoal always disposed of his ballads to the profession directly; that is, without the intervention of a middleman, and on several occasions he was known to have secured a slight loan in advance on the promise of a song (he was merchant enough to discount his notes), and all this, I think, argues a remote acquaintance, at least, with the profession.

Be this as it may, the afternoon of that same day found Charcoal in the private office of a variety theatre, well patronized by the respectable middle classes. In the gaudily furnished room he looked for all the world like a picture of poverty done in oil, and painted to adorn by contrast the parlors of the rich. The manager, a shrewd, bright, dapper little fellow, read the ballad quickly, and recognizing in it the element of popularity, made an offer of four dollars to the author. The author timidly suggested that it might be worth five; a ticket for the next Saturday night's performance was thrown in as a kind of "split the difference," and the bargain was concluded.

"Under what name do you wish it to appear?" asked the purchaser.

"Name?" Charcoal snapped his fingers melodramatically. "What did he care for a name? his name was Charcoal; if he called himself by any other, he would be called a liar. It's money, money he wants," and he jingled his four dollars most musically to his own ears, at least, and left.

Between that afternoon and the next Saturday the ballad—I forgot to mention that Charcoal entitled his effort, "The Same Old Tune"—became the rage; everybody whistled it, from musician to merchant, and from merchant to cab-driver. Those who could not whistle hummed, and those who could neither hum nor whistle sang the air. However, the ballad had not yet become unpopular from over-popularity; and had the author's name been appended the world would have sung his praises as well as his music, but since it appeared anonymously, no one stopped to inquire the name of the composer.

On the night of that memorable Saturday of which I speak, Charcoal scaled the dizzy heights of the *paradiso*, and waited patiently amid the impatient gods for the rising of the curtain.   He wondered what these same gods—who edged away from him as though he were a leprous mortal—would have said, had they known that he was the writer of the song which had set the world astir.   A voice within him called loudly, "Announce yourself! announce yourself! Get up and say, I am the author of 'The Same Old Tune;'" but he throttled the voice and sat in silence, so depressed by the company of his own gloomy thoughts that he could not enter into the spirit necessary for the enjoyment of the performance.

The sudden appearance of Mlle. de Moreau, such was her *nom de programme*, called him with a rude shock from the depths of his dungeons in Spain to the higher world of realities. A look of profound surprise crossed his face; his lips rounded as if to give vent to an "O;" he shielded his eyes from the glare of the lights with his hands, and craned his neck to see better.

She sang his song in a clear, sweet soprano voice which brought out the pathos of the story so well that the audience was moved to the very depths and cheered itself hoarse. Not Charcoal, however; he preserved a stolid silence, and sat as if carved of stone. Perhaps he had exhausted all his emotion in writing the song, and hence could not be moved by hearing it sung; perhaps this may have been the prima donna referred to by Kid Kelly, and he may have been thinking of the strange pranks destiny plays; perhaps,—but why waste more time in useless conjecture?

One thing is certain: this actress, painted,

powdered, ornamented with a lavish display of cheap jewelry; this thing of shreds and patches seemed as beautiful to Charcoal as did Beatrice, clad in saintly garb, surrounded by choiring angels, and refulgent with celestial light, to the inspired vision of Dante.

And lo! he, Charcoal, the miserable tramp, the lackey for thieves and outcasts, had poured out this finest thought and most soulful melody, by means of which she moved this large audience to tears and plaudits and wild acclaim.

Lackey for tramps!—if right were his, he should be leader of men of thought and fancy. Oh, the pity of it!—to be so much above the life he was leading, and yet be bound there by the iron chain of circumstance. The bathos, the eternal unfitness of things held him on the balance, trembling between laughter and tears; lost opportunities, wasted life, talents scattered to the four winds, surged before him in dread visual images that grasped him, as it were, by the throat and left him breathless.

He yearned for the slums, he would fit

more naturally into that horrible niche of
creation, he would be more in harmony with
the *ensemble* of his surroundings. He arose
to leave.

Once out however, he regretted his departure bitterly and longed to return. The
lights, the crowd, the music, the enthusiasm, the bare stage itself, had exerted a
powerful fascination on his feverish imagination. "Go back to the slums?" His higher
self, his *alter ego* was up in arms against the
proposition.

The passers-by cast pitying glances at
him as he moved along; such a miserable,
wretched, dejected, poverty-stricken mortal
did he seem. He had never heeded those
glances before, or rather they had become
so common that they made no impression
on his consciousness; now they aroused his
anger. He wanted admiration, not pity;
he had done great things; if they only knew,
he was the author of "The Same Old
Tune." A dark alley offered friendly con-
cealment, and he turned thither with hurried
step.

As he passed the stage door, for this blind alley led to the stage door, the actors were filing down the passage in groups of twos and threes. A desire to see again the prima donna, who had interpreted his song so feelingly, arrested his steps; he hid against the projecting wall and waited.

The stage mechanics came out in a body, went their way, and left the alley to silence, to him and the faint light that flickered over the entrance.

The door opened again, and a woman tripped up a few stairs. There she was! Charcoal sprang forward only to stare a startled *coryphée* in the face. The poor *danseuse* ran down the alley at a pace that bade defiance to all the conventional rules of her art. Frightened, disappointed, but not discouraged he pressed back again. She was long in coming, but he did not mind that; for the night might as well be passed here as elsewhere. He began to fear lest she had left before his advent, or slipped away under his very nose into the darkness. This fear crossed his mind, just as Mlle. de

Moreau and her escort passed the door-way —the escort was a contingency upon which he had not reckoned.

Charcoal crouched down and debated with himself whether he should speak or not; he was so near that he could touch her with his elbow, and yet he seemed to see her through the halo of an interminable distance. "If I could only speak to her for five minutes face to face as that man was doing!"

They scolded a second or two because the carriage was late, and then the conversation, evidently begun indoors, drifted to the mystery attending the authorship of that wonderful song.

"Yes, I should like to meet the man who had sentiment and feeling enough to write that song; I have an idea that the man who wrote it is—" The noise of clattering hoofs drowned her last words, and Charcoal could not hear them, hard as he tried. The carriage stopped with a loud "whoa" from the coachman.

He must speak now or never; the pangs of authorship were upon him and he plunged forward, "Madame, I, Char—Ben Latham, I am the author of 'The Same Old Tune.'" She shrieked and jumped into the carriage. Was it the name or the sudden appearance of such a character in such a place, at such a time, that frightened Mlle. de Moreau?

The escort lifted his cane, then, seeing the humor of the situation, and thinking the joke too good to go unpaid, he flung the vagabond a dime; and the carriage rolled along.

Charcoal let the dime lie where it fell and scornfully hurried away; afterwards he slunk back, poked in the mud, and clutched the coin that he had spurned.

Fame has its rewards.

A Coat of One Color

"Timeo Danaos et dona ferentes"—
Look a gift horse in the mouth.

No one ever learned how Whitey became the owner of his silk hat and his long blue coat, made *á la Russe*, sable lined and sable trimmed; but the most stupid should have known that he did not come by them honestly, for should he wear what were honestly his, then the rascal's skin would have shielded him but poorly from the heat of summer and the winter's cold.

According to one of his accounts—and his accounts varied with his audience—he was the seventh son of a seventh son, and born with a cowl on his face; and the coat and hat, more particularly the coat, became his by the sacred law of septogeniture.

He boasted that it was in his power to influence the destinies of men for good or evil,

55

as he chose, since the heritage endowed the seventh son with the divine gift of working miracles and gave him absolute control over all the demons of the lower regions and all the angels of the higher.

The seventh son (I go back a generation), whoever the venerable gentleman may have been, was certainly careful of his clothes; for the coat showed not a sign of wear, and the beaver was as polished as if it had just left the hatter's block.

Whitey declared that with the clothes on his will was omnipotent; but with them off, he was as impotent, as ordinarily mortal as Hercules in the Centaur's deadly robe. You may be sure that he was never caught napping or awake without these precious garments. All of his sacred person that he exposed to vulgar gaze, his cheeks, leprously white from disease, and his hawk-like nose and dreamy eyes,—what occultist has not dreamy eyes and a hawk-like nose?—which peeped forth from the loophole made by the space between the collar of his coat and the rim of his hat.

Among the crowd of superstitious crimi-
nals at The Lucky Number there was but a
handful that was skeptical of his power to influence the fates to apportion more weal and
less woe, or more woe and less weal, as the
case might be, in the destinies of their lives;
and these, save one, he gradually won to
belief by the use of *verba sesquipedalia*, by
sleight of hand tricks, and a few bold predic-
tions that, as luck would have it, came to pass.

What is more convincing to the ignorant
and the superstitious than the esoteric clad in
high-sounding, empty phraseology? The
poor gudgeons nibbled at his bait without
suspicion, and when they had nibbled long
enough to be caught by the hook, he drew
them in remorselessly.

His success made the charlatan arrogant
to the degree of insolence; he threatened to
visit them all with ills that made the plagues
of Pharaoh seem blessings by comparison;
and when they were quaking with fear, he
seized the propitious moment and declared
himself the Czar of The Lucky Number.
His realm to be sure was not vast, but the

very narrowness of its confines (there is no disadvantage without some contingent advantage) aided him in the establishment of an unlimited monarchy and allowed him to rule his subjects with a rod of iron.

Then the man of magic grew exorbitant in his demands, as is natural for one who has risen from tenement to throne with such Mercurial rapidity, and he imposed even upon the nobility the most menial of tasks. His peasantry were taxed to the utmost that he might have *vodka* in superabundance,—by the canfuls; and once, when the taxes had yielded beyond precedent, he gave forth the ukase that his shoes be blacked.

Human forbearance has limits beyond which no one may venture to pass, but the autocrat disregarded all boundary lines and encroached on the interior. The ukase was such a flagrant abuse of power that even Charcoal, the most timid serf in the realm, upon whom the whole weight of the imperial edict fell, openly refused to obey its behest.

The nobility and *muzhiks* surreptitiously countenanced the revolt of the serf, mur-

murs portentous of a terrible revolution filled the air; the ruler felt his throne (a chair minus its cane bottom) totter, and under his breath he prayed, "God save the czar."

A great emergency surely, but with a majesty equal to it he arose from his throne. Crafty potentate that he was, in peace he had prepared himself for war; while sitting supinely on his throne he had been dreaming of a great revolt, and mentally outlining a course that should crush it at a single blow, though it have as many heads as a hydra, and each head be endowed with as many lives as a cat.

He removed his crown and threw his imperial mantle from off his shoulders. Think of it, the mystical garments of his father, the original seventh son, thrown angrily on the floor by his seventh son!

"Knave, take them and they are yours," he exclaimed, "but if you so much as touch the sacred hem of that garment with the tip of a finger, you bring upon yourself the anathema of the seventh son. The anathema of the seventh son, I warn you!"

He spoke with a sublimity befitting a monarch; Tom Keene, as Richelieu, never shook altitudinous galleries with such a thunder.

And Charcoal, you think, shrinking back in fear, craved pardon, and let the crown and mantle lie where they fell? Not much! Charcoal was a poet, you remember, and hence not to be browbeaten out of a sable coat and a silk hat even by the anathematization of one seven times removed from the seventh son. Charcoal was "the one" who had steadfastly remained a skeptic; while not having the physical courage to declare his dissension openly, he had the mental courage to remain unconvinced by the rhodomontade of this hoax. Fearful that his prize might be taken from him, he pulled the hat over his ears, grasped the coat tightly, and hastened out of doors.

And the Czar, you think, bemoaned his lost finery, and repented his rash act? If so you mistake again; it was just what he had expected; it was just what he had planned. Before the night came he would again

ascend his throne in triumph; and this nihil-
ist, this skeptic, who was ever a menace to
his reign, this Gringoire of the gutters,
would drag his lengthening chains Siberia-
ward and cast more than one longing,
lingering look behind.

"He will regret his foolhardiness; the
curse of the seventh son is on his shoulders.
The hat and coat will float back to me
through the realms of space, and this rebel
will beg me to release him from his dungeon
by my magic. But he will beg in vain, in
vain," and the wizard stalked out of the
place, majestic even in his rags.

Charcoal moved through the wind-swept
streets; and in the intense cold he revelled
in the sensation of feeling warm, a sensation
he had not experienced for years. Clothes
do not make the man, but he was only half
a man, and the clothes supplying the missing half, made him one, for the nonce, without disputing the axiom. People turned
around to look at him with an air which
said, "Who is that aristocrat?"

To say that he walked along proud as a

peacock, would phrase it by only a half; but since nothing is known that walks prouder than a peacock, his pride must be allowed to go half unexpressed.

In one of the pockets he found a nickel, the discovery made him jubilant; it might be the coat of Fortunatas, as well as that of the seventh son. He plunged in the same pocket again and found nothing—the coat belonged to the seventh son only, curse it! Then he began a painstaking search, and all he got for his pains was a letter, sealed carefully and addressed in a neat hand.

Charcoal was about to open the envelope and read the letter, when he reflected that he might gain more by handing it to the person addressed; for, if the seal were broken, he dared not deliver it; and, in case the contents proved worthless, he would defraud himself in two ways. Why gratify a vulgar curiosity when an emolument was at stake? He was a poet, a man of high ideals, and the seal on a letter was a sacred thing in his eyes.

The writer of sentimental ballads buttoned

his coat and hurried on; "Mr. Von Million, President of the Tenth National Bank," said he, repeating the address, "I wonder if the gentleman is distantly related to Whitey." He might be one of the other six brothers, or one of the six brothers of the seventh son, for, in a family of such complicated relationship, one might easily claim blood ties with anybody one chose.

"The letter may bring me in a fortune of itself," he reflected; "what a gudgeon Whitey is to think I would take a bluff like that."

"What a gudgeon that balladmonger is to have called my bluff," thought the wizard, when shivering in the cold he saw Charcoal replace the letter and make rapid strides, as he surmised, towards the place to which it was addressed. They both fostered the same high opinion of each other's worth; which is easily understood, if one stops to consider that both poet and magician work in the same material, the immaterial.

Charcoal's dress admitted him into the president's office without delay and the unrolling of yards of red tape. "As this world runs," he mused, "a man should always go well dressed."

With a bow that would have won the admiration of a dancing master, Mr. Von Million, taking the letter, asked the bearer to be seated. "The materialism of our day," ran Charcoal's thoughts, "is enough to make a good poet a bad pessimist; more respect is paid to a wearer of sables than to a writer of sonnets."

The president's face changed color as he read, he gasped for breath and nervously crumpled the paper in his hand. "The communication must be important," concluded the balladmonger; Charcoal had all the sensitive intuition of a bard; the note, for it was a simple note and not a letter, read: "Unless you deliver the bearer 15,000 dollars immediately, he will blow your brains out." The communication was important.

"I will be back with the money in a minute," said the terrified capitalist in a voice that tried hard to betray no feeling of fear, and he stepped towards the door on tip-toe, as if he were afraid of the sound of his foot-fall.

"I wonder where the man lives to whom I am to take the money. But what's the difference? No matter where he lives, I can deliver it in a minute; it's all one to me"— Charcoal showed a true poet's carelessness in money affairs.

If he should hand him 5,000 dollars, if it be that much, he would buy him a Sabine farm, and in the center of it, on the sloping bank of an artificial lake (a thing beautiful to behold in the summertime, when the water lilies were in full bloom, and the swans went swimming between the small wooded islands) he would build him, *O sancta simplicitas*, a log cabin; and therein would he devote the rest of his days to the muses, and to gazing out of the window on the waters of his lake, shimmering in the moonlight, for inspiration.

And if it were 10,000 dollars? With the other five he would build a barn of brown stone with pressed brick trimmings, and stock it with blooded Kentucky horses, and gorgeous turnouts, and colored footmen and coachmen, who should be clad in top boots, tight-fitting knee-breeches of white, coats of flaming red, and black silk hats with white bands and cockades of yellow.

When the weather was fine he might, by way of diversion, drive to the city and stop his coach and four at The Lucky Number for refreshment. Would the hobos recognize their former frater in poverty in this grand gentleman, who carelessly threw a silver dollar on the bar for a schooner of beer, and refused the change? He felt sure that they would not. But if they did, there would be such a sensation as one sees only in a melodrama.

Charcoal slipped down in the upholstered chair, and, stretching his feet out towards the fire that burned cheerfully in the grate, he added story after story to his castles in Spain. How pleasant it is to build castles when one has lived in a dungeon all one's life.

Between the heat blazed out from the grate

and the warmth engendered by his sable, he found himself uncomfortable, and absent-mindedly, dreaming still of his castle (it had assumed the proportions of a sky-scraper by this time), he arose, removed his heavy overcoat, and threw it across the back of the chair.

The sight of his rags threw him from the window of the top story of his castle of dreams to terra firma of the actual and the present; he awoke with a start, and, blaming himself for his folly, he was about to don the robe again when the president entered the room, holding in his hand a small white canvas bag. He dropped the bag on the table with a thud and remarked, "It's all in fifty dollar gold pieces."

Charcoal jumped to grab it; a policeman entered from another door, and grabbed Charcoal. "Whitey, the letter, and the coat, damn them! I see his game," he maundered.

In the twinkling of a star his fortune, baseless fabric, had vanished into nothingness; but his dreams, substantial gift of the muses, still remained, and as long as they were his he could be rich as a Crœsus, in his mind.

One guardian of the peace had just assisted the poet into the patrol wagon, and another guardian of order, who carried in his hands the hat and coat that had cost Charcoal his liberty, was about to mount its steps when he felt two quick, sudden jerks. He turned swiftly, but too slowly; the hat and coat were gone. He caught a glimpse of the thief disappearing in the crowd and gave chase. "No use," said the officer returning to the wagon breathless and empty-handed, "that fellow is made of rubber and lightning."

The patrol had not yet passed the door of The Lucky Number when the Czar entered; his white face was wreathed in a happy smile, his beaver sat crown-like on his head, and his person was arrayed in the glory of his sable coat.

"Where's Charcoal?" they asked.

"Going over the road," he answered indifferently, "see, there he goes."

They ran to the window; they looked

at each other in amazement, as men who have seen a great miracle performed and who have not yet recovered from the effect.

"How did that happen?" one bolder than the rest ventured to ask.

"As I told you it would happen," thundered the wizard; "he dared to touch the sacred coat of the seventh son."

"After this," he said autocratically, "I want my boots blacked every morning; you may take turns."

They quarreled among themselves for the honor of the first shine.

A Pair of Eyes

THE Doctor, the Quill, and the Lark, arm in arm, staggered out of the low doorway of The Lucky Number, the vilest saloon in the slums. A veritable triangle of vice these three, held together by sympathetic lines of sin, debauchery and crime. As they emerged from the doorway,—their sodden, leering countenances made more grewsome by the thin, flickering, bluish light puffed about them by the single gas jet which hung overhead,—they formed a group as shockingly realistic as a painting by Jean Beraud.

The Doctor, whom the cheap drink had merely inflamed to madness, maintained his equilibrium without difficulty on the outside; the Quill, who was just sober enough to know where he was going, stumbled along on the inside; and the Lark, who had more than he was able to carry, wisely choosing the center, was supported by the other two.

Thus balanced, the trio reached their lodging, a miserable bare hole on the top floor of the poorest tenement in the whole neighborhood.

The climbing of stairs was an obstacle on which the Lark had not reckoned, but he finally managed to overcome it with the assistance of the Quill's strong arm and the Doctor's violent blows and loud curses.

The Doctor, fumbling around in the darkness, found and lit a candle. Few words are needed to describe what the rays of light from that candle fell upon,—squalor, dirt, and utter bareness tell all. The Lark felt, by a kind of instinct, that he was at home, and dropped on the floor in a stupor. The Doctor seized the single stool for himself, used his own leg for its missing third, and sat there, resting his fat chin on his hand. The Quill was preparing to squat on the floor, after the example set by the Lark, when a vigorous kick from the Doctor's unoccupied member aroused him.

"Wait a minute, you, I have something to say."

These words seemed to carry all the authority of superior brute force; for the one commanded rubbed his eyes vigorously and tried to sit upright. His first attempt failed, but the threatening boot of the Doctor was too powerful a stimulus to make a third necessary.

"Have you any money?"

The Quill looked up in a manner that plainly interrogated the Doctor's sanity. Money, could a man buy whiskey for two such thirsty birds and keep his money too? He had merely learned the art of forgery, never that of magic.

"Stop your crazy tongue and search the Lark."

The innermost recesses of the sleeper's pockets did not reveal a sou to the Quill's investigation.

"Bah!" snapped the commander, "his songs are stale, they are as worn out as the rags on his filthy body." This was a reference to the sentimental ditties by which the

once tuneful voice of the Lark had enticed
stray pennies from the fallen women of the
slums, who gave rather in the hope of col-
lecting principal and interest from the Lord
than as a reward to the singer — "who
giveth to the poor—"

"And that damned pen of yours has n't
turned in a penny for months! You coward,
you 're afraid to forge again; I've a mind to
pitch you out of the window." The Doctor arose in his drunken wrath, and the
Quill crept close to the wall in craven fear.

"Look here, this thing must stop; it 's
gone on long enough, I'm tired of hoaxing
fools with my magic cures just to support
two such lazy vagabonds in luxury. It's
time you were helping me, and one of you
is going to help me, you hear!"

The vender of magic cures sat lost in
meditation for a few seconds, and then burst
out in a torrent of vile oaths,—the puddles
of the gutter pouring into a sewer.

"I have a new song for our Lark to sing,
and one that will catch pennies by the handful: 'Mister, help a poor blind man;' "—he

chuckled this last phrase in a falsetto voice, and holding his hand out pleadingly, shut his eyes to imitate a figure in a picture that flashed over his brain, maddened to frenzy by liquor. "There you, take this."

The erstwhile forger, held upright by the sheer strength of fear, picked up the rusty knife flung on the floor.

"Take that blanket and cut it in strips."

"For what?"

"For what, you drunken fool; since when must I give you reasons? Do you want to go on the streets and work?"

The forger shuddered at the prospect— "God forbid."

"Well, then do as I say."

His fingers moved as fast as an incipient attack of delirium tremens would permit, but not fast enough to suit his majesty. "Will you work, you, or must I help?" he shrieked. This proffer of assistance had the desired effect,—the menial's increased activity made aid unnecessary.

"Now bind his hands and his feet tight, tight as you can!"

He bent over the sleeping singer of ditties and carried out the stern command, wondering, but not daring to ask, what his master intended to do.

The master satisfied himself that the task was thoroughly done, and then bestowed a kick upon his servant for reward; he added the finishing touch himself by stuffing a filthy rag in the mouth of the unfortunate drunkard.

A loathsome for boding made the Quill's flesh creep; his teeth chattered, his nerves quivered and twitched, and his legs seemed to be giving way from beneath him. He ventured a faint remonstrance.

The scampering of a rat threw a lump of loose plaster on the floor, the candle spluttering went out, and the frightened rat squeaked. Through his rounded lips the Doctor blew a long, deep-drawn "w-h-e-w."

"Ghosts, ghosts!" gasped the delirious Quill, crawling to the Doctor on his hands and knees, and clinging to him for protection; "ghosts, they want me, they are going to choke me, they have their damned hands on my throat! For God's sake, light the candle and scare them away!''

This pitiful fright afforded the Doctor infinite amusement, and he laughed fiendishly. ''Scare them away nothing, I'll call them here by the dozens. W-hew, w-h-e-w, I'll have them tear you to shreds unless you mind me, and do what I say, and stop your crazy chatter. W-h-e-w!''

''Yes, I'll do anything, anything; I'll kill myself if you want—only hurry, hurry; the nasty things have their fingers on my throat,'' he gurgled.

Too much fear was as bad as too little; the man might faint dead away and become useless. So thinking, the Doctor struck a match to light the candle again.

In obedience to the order of his master, the Quill heated a long thin wire until it turned white in the flames of the candle.

''Now burn his eyes out,'' commanded the monster.

The Quill darted to the door, and was out before the Doctor could stop him. The revolting fiendishness of the purpose shocked him into soberness; it acted like a sudden plunge into freezing water.

The lion missed the jackal and cursed him with a roar of angry oaths. "It's better after all," he muttered. "I can do the job myself, and get everything that's in it; besides, if I am found out, I can lay the whole business on him."

Intense, unbearable pain aroused the Lark from his drunken stupor, but his pain gave way to terror when he discovered that his hands and feet were bound tightly. He lay still for a few minutes trying to account for it all; finding himself unable to do so, his distress increased, a sense of the supernatural fell upon him, he reached out to shake the Doctor. The Doctor awoke, his teeth chattering with the cold; "What do you want?" he growled; "do'nt you think it's hard enough for a restless man to sleep in the cold, and with the rats gnawing away, without being disturbed by a maniac?"

"What has happened,—why am I bound like this? What does it mean?"

"Ask the Quill, he knows and I do'nt! Let me sleep, you hear!"

The Lark began jerking around the room on his knees in a pathetic search for the Quill.

The Quill had gone, what did that mean? Why had he sneaked away like a door-mat* in the night?

"You will find out soon enough," said the Doctor grimly, and fell asleep again.

The Lark's torture became excruciating; it seemed to him that someone was boring into his eyes with an auger of interminable length, and that the laceration grew more unendurable at every twist of the flesh-rending tool. He moaned and groaned, but to him the Doctor paid no heed. A weird, harrowing apprehension, more insufferable because less palpable than his cruciation, mastered him now. He was like a whipped child thrust into the darkness—smart and ache became as naught in comparison with the dread of shrieking goblins, hideous dwarfs and revengeful giants, with which

*A sneak thief.

the frightened child's imagination peoples the darkness. The Lark could stand it no longer, and for the sake of companionship, for the mere soothing sensation of hearing a human voice, he aroused the Doctor.

By this time the room was suffused with the light of early morn, just tinted by the red gleam of the winter's sun, struggling with the dissipated darkness. The Doctor did not seem at all unwilling to rise, he was even so good-natured that he whistled an air while completing his toilet, which consisted in rubbing his face with his hands and shaking his clothes.

The Lark ventured on a question: "What time is it?"

"Breakfast time, without the breakfast," was the answer.

"But man, you 're jesting; it's dark yet."

"Dark nothing, it's light as day. Do you think it's going to stay dark forever? Can't you tell time without a thimble* ?"

The Lark trembled from head to foot;

*A watch.

what had happened dawned upon him in a flash. Timidly he framed the words and slowly, like one who wishes to be disputed in what he affirms; "Am I—" somehow the last word would not out.

The Doctor was not so fearful. "Yes, undoubtedly he had lost his sight; too much drink, and cheap drink at that, had done the work." He had seen cases like it before in his short, mundane existence.

It would have moved a hangman to tears to have seen how the wretched sufferer staggered and collapsed under this fiendish blow.

The Doctor laughed. "What is the use of carrying on so; what does sight profit a man who has not the money necessary to see things?"

The Lark evidently found no consolation in the Doctor's philosophy; for he howled and kicked the floor in impotent rage.

The Doctor dealt him a violent clout and threatened to desert him if he did n't "cease his music."

"What, would you leave me to starve to death like a rat in a trap?" he asked.

"Not so long as you behave yourself. Come, it's time to go to work."

"Work, to work, what can I do?"

"Basket* and crutch it.† "

The blood shot to the Lark's head, his skull felt as if cleaved by the blow of an axe, and he fell on the floor in a swoon.

* * * *

The Doctor led the Lark homeward against a chill penetrating north wind. They were both numb with cold and trudged on through the snow in silence, not wanting to drain by speech the little vitality left them. The Doctor, who had watched the blind man closely from the shelter of a doorway, was not quite so exhausted and spoke first.

"How much?" the question was laconic, the answer was still more so—"Nothing."

"Not a red?"

"Not a red!"

The tyrant raged, his anger carried him beyond himself: had they not been in the street—well, it was good for him that

*Beg from house to house.
†Beg on the streets.

they were where they could be seen and heard! So, not a red, and how long was this to continue? How long was he to support a worthless, blind beggar in idleness? It was the same yesterday; and the day before, not enough to buy them a decent meal. Bah! he could do better alone! He was playing out, he was getting stale.

The Lark never answered a word; for one reason, not knowing what to answer; for another reason, not daring to answer anything.

The Doctor, foreign to his habit, repeated; "You are getting stale, you are played out! I have a quarter left, enough to buy supper and bed for one, and you can go to the devil—it is the devil that cares for the blind anyway."

There was a crisp sound of hurrying feet breaking through the frozen snow, and the Lark stood alone. The last stunning blow was struck so unexpectedly that a few minutes passed before the wretched beggar recovered from his dazed condition and realized what had happened. But when he did realize it, the cowardice, the revolting cruelty of the desertion sickened him to the last degree; he was nauseated. If his tormentor before leaving had only been considerate enough to have ended his miserable existence, the Lark would not have thought him so heartless; but to leave him quivering and gasping like that,— it destroyed even the Lark's faith in human depravity.

Blind, freezing, starving, penniless, shelterless, friendless, deserted—there was but one thing for him to do, to finish what the Doctor had left undone.

Twice every day, once when departing and once when returning to his lodgings, he passed over the bridge; hence, naturally enough, the river stood out prominently in the foreground of his kaleidoscopic vision of death and suicide. He trusted in his sense of direction to lead him due west along the half mile line that lay between him and the river. His point of departure was a corner formed by six streets intersecting one another, and without any hesitancy he chose the one going due north—the sixth sense has its illusions as well as the other five.

He was sure that he had covered his half mile twice, and he stopped, wondering why he heard none of those peculiarly hollow and jangled sounds which had always apprised him of the proximity of the bridge. Possibly he might have taken the wrong road, he would wait until some passer-by came along and find out to a certainty. But the passer-by was long in coming, in fact, he came not at all; and no wonder, for the Lark had halted at the foot of an open plot of ground that marked the end of the dark, unfrequented short street. In a less excitable mood of mind, the absence of all traffic would have indicated his mistake to him before he had proceeded a quarter of the distance.

The thermometer was falling rapidly, and with it the temperature of his blood was falling; if he stood still much longer the cold might prove a bad substitute for the water. The Lark preferred drowning to freezing. Possibly his anxiety to reach his destination had made him cover the road far more quickly in imagination than he could in actuality; so thinking he started forward. His will was stronger than his weak, starved, over-worked, fatigued body (and that few minutes' pause had brought home to him how fatigued and over-worked it was), and he fell headlong into the snow. He tried to rise, but the inertia of his flesh outweighed the power of his muscle. He would rest a few seconds, gather his strength and try again.

The wind settled to a dead calm and the night air turned biting cold; I say biting cold, for the Lark felt as if it had sharp, savage teeth that tore into his flesh and laid his bones bare. So stiff and numb did his body grow that he found himself unable to bend his leg or move his arm. The pain he suffered on that terrible night when he had lost his sight seemed trifling in comparison with what he was now undergoing.

Gradually he lost all sensation; one might have stuck pins into him and they would not have been felt. A stupor, an indescribable drowsiness, made him desire to sleep; he knew the danger of such a sleep, and tried to ward it off; but a sudden, thrilling, genial warmth passed through him and made the temptation irresistible: giving way to it, he was soon at rest.

Towards morning the calm broke; a stiff, blustering wind veered from the south, and the cold retreated slowly before a storm of snow which sent flakes, long and curly as the feathers of a moulting goose, whirling to the ground. A shroud, soft and light as eiderdown, was woven around the frozen body of the Lark, but an envious gust of wind seized and tore it to shreds. Only one small square patch of the covering escaped destruction, and strangely enough, —rude sarcasm of the elements!—that patch hid the Lark's mendicant sign:

"I am blind! Please help me!"

The Magic Herb

"Albeit for profit and lucre all things are set to sale."—HOLINSHED.

The Doctor took his degree of M.D. in the easiest way imaginable, he conferred it upon himself; or rather he was graduated from a college of which he was the founder, and the faculty and committee on degrees.

The curriculum of the college, like the Doctor, was original and unique; you might compare all the catalogues of all the colleges in the world, and not find a course of studies bearing the faintest resemblance to the one his offered. The reason is not far to seek, the Doctor's college had no curriculum.

His peculiar school of medicine could easily claim two advantages over every other school; it required no laborious preparation for entrance, it insisted upon no arduous application for graduation. I forgot a third advantage and the greatest; it made the study of *materia medica* so easy that a child could grasp all the intricacies of that difficult subject in less than a week. For, according to the Doctor's way of thinking, there was but one healing property in all nature, and that property was contained in the resurrection plant.

To know this plant thoroughly was to know everything worth the knowing in medicine; because this magic herb, as he termed it, was a cure for all the ills that flesh is heir to, — nature's sweet restorer, a veritable panacea, in short, it was medicine. How simple does the complicated science of healing become with the discovery of a panacea.

The Doctor boasted that he was the discoverer of the precious boon to suffering humanity, and he therefore deemed himself entitled to an honorary degree.

As the name would signify, the resurrection plant is in truth a miracle of nature; it dies and comes to life again, or, to be more exact, it never dies. When dried out, when every particle of moisture has been consumed, its fronds shrivel and curl convulsively about the centre, forming a small ball of a dead brown color; but only a few minutes after the plant is watered the fronds uncurl, spread out to the light, and become beautiful in their coat of lustrous green.

The Doctor charged his patients ten cents for a magic herb; he charged them nothing for his call.   Compare the cures he effected with the paltry honorarium he received, and you must admit that the Doctor was a humanitarian; he was a martyr as well, in as much as he was a humanitarian against his will.   The discoverer of the panacea was mercenary; he longed for riches, but people persisted in misunderstanding his motives, and crowning him a philanthropist.   The world has ever misunderstood its greatest characters.

To have philanthropy thrust upon you in this fashion is exasperating, and the Doctor chafed continually under the burden of his unsought glory. Every time that he received his beggarly stipend (and every time that he did n't receive it), he forgot his professional dignity and relieved his injured feelings in curses that would have aroused the envy of a trooper.

Once in his life, once only, and then at the very outset of his career, did he receive a fee in any way commensurate with what he thought his worth; and he would have abandoned the practice of medicine in disgust, but the hope, ever floating before his eyes like a will-o'-the-wisp, of gaining another such emolument allured him so far into the swamps of beggardom that he found it impossible to extricate himself. This particular fee played such an important part in the Doctor's history; he planned and schemed to gain it with such astuteness, worthy of a better cause, that—but thereby hangs my tale.

There was a rumor current in the neighborhood that a certain Ann Garsch, a half-witted German seamstress, had by dint of rigid economy and ceaseless industry laid away a big pot of money for a rainy day.

When the rumor reached his ears, the avaricious leech, fearful lest the pot might

disappear before his appearance, lost not a
second in posting thither. A half-witted
woman, he figured, could be bled far easier
than one with a full measure of wit. Herein
his reckoning was at fault; what Ann Garsch
lacked in wit she made up in parsimony.
She was rather monomaniac than half-witted,
and her monomania was saving.

"Miss," began the crafty physician,
"do n't you want to buy a magic herb?"

He started to enumerate its long list of
virtues, when she interrupted, "Does it cost
anything?"

"Only a dime," he said seductively,
"and — "

"Then I do n't want it; go 'long."

"Do you expect me to give 'em away?"
he snarled, "I 'm selling 'em now for half
what they cost me, and a quarter of what
they 're worth."

"Yer a fool then, go 'long."

The door had scarcely slammed before the
Doctor forgot himself and his professional
dignity, "She may have a pot of money,
but I 'll bet the lid is soldered to the pot so

tight that you can't get it off with a crow-bar.''

However, he did not lose all courage; he felt as sure that this toiling seamstress had money as that a spinning spider makes a web; nay, he was as sure that she had money as that she had life, and why should a physician of his ability give up hope before life is extinct and money gone?

He allowed a whole month to elapse before he called again, in order that she might forget the unfavorable impression made by his first visit; but in that period the Doctor did not stand idly counting the minutes as they glided away into the past. From the assiduity with which he collected facts and incidents relating to Ann Garsch's life, you might have thought this humble seamstress was a character of vital import-ance in present history, and that he wished to write a biography which should be stand-ard for all generations to come.

From one source he learnt that the per-sistent efforts of the Salvation Army had recently won her for a convert, and that she

was now austerely religious,—a characteristic
well worth the remembering, and he jotted
it down on his mental note book with a blue
pencil. From another source he learnt that
the seamstress's lover had deserted her
and their little child over a year ago, and
that she was waiting with yearning heart for
the day that should bring him back; these
data he wrote down in red ink. From a
third source he learnt that the Quill was the
woman's quondam lover; a fact so important that it could be remembered without
any notation.

When the Doctor visited Ann Garsch for
the second time, he had formulated a different line of attack against the stronghold of
her purse.

"It is in my power to bring your lover
to you again," were his first words.

The coat she was basting slipped from
her hands and fell on the floor as she stared
at him with her large eyes, vacant as painted
eyes on a painted face.

"Do it, then, do it; in the name of heaven,
do," she pleaded, the corners of her weak,

sensual mouth quivering with nervous excitement. "It will cost money," was his brutal reply, "for I'm poor and need money."

Her eyes lit with an intelligent shrewdness. "How do you know that I have a lover?"

"How do I know?" he exclaimed, "how do I know a thousand things? How do I know that your mother's name was Johanna Melzer, that you were her third child? How do I know that you were born in Hamburg and came to this country when you were ten, and that you will be twenty-eight on the fourth of January? How do I know the Quill is the father of that child," —he pointed scornfully to the old-fashioned German cradle in which her child was sleeping peacefully. "How? because my magic herb gives me the power to read the secrets of the mind. Now do you believe that I can bring your lover back?"

The clairvoyancy of this uncanny reader of minds made her shudder; his divinations struck with an accumulative horror, the first

making her marvel, the last causing her flesh
to creep.   She felt a desire to run away, to
crawl within herself, that she might escape
what must be the malign influence of his
hypnotic will.

"How much will it cost?" she asked
tremulously.

"One hundred dollars," he answered
boldly.   The price was tentative, the sor-
cerer was willing to take less, he would not
refuse more.

If a beggar stopping you on the street
should extend his hand piteously and ask
for one hundred dollars, you could not be
more surprised than she at the value the
Doctor placed on his services; to her a dollar did not represent ten dimes, it represented ten coats, and ten coats represented
almost two days of agonizing labor.   Her
table of money was not computed in cents
and dimes, but in thread and stitches.   One
hundred dollars was Ann's fortune; for
three years she had been nibbling bit by bit
from her diurnal pittance of seventy cents
to accumulate the sum.

What sacrifice, what self-abnegation, what toil — toil that bends the back, dims the eye and wears the thumb to bone — did this one hundred dollars not symbolize?   It was a seignorage that body and soul demanded from comfort, health and happiness for the turning of flesh and blood into coin.

"Very well," answered the seamstress, calmly, "I will give you fifty dollars now, and the other fifty on the day when he comes back to me and the child."

O Misery and Want, how can you love so much!

"Fool," reflected he, "you might just as well have gotten two hundred."   Doubtless had he been alone his professional dignity would have been forgotten again.   Straightway he unrolled a brown plant from a mass of rags and papers, and placed it carefully on the floor; then he knelt and spread his hands over it in silent benediction.

The benediction done, the Doctor, in a low voice raised gradually to a higher and higher key, began an incantation, metered, monotoned; and his body swayed back and forth in rhythmical unison with its measure. There came a pause in his abracadabra, "Kneel down in prayer," he cried thrillingly, and set his body oscillating slowly from right to left as he modulated the sing-song of his incantation to a subdued, faint tone.

His gibberish ran through the threnody of her prayer like a motif through the orchestration of a mournful overture.

To the ignorant, superstitious seamstress, the Doctor's rigmarole appealed with all the impelling force of the unknowable and the sublime.   Terrified, she tried to turn her eyes from him, but he held them in control as irresistibly as if they were attached to his hands by wires.

At first perfunctory, her prayer—as the supernatural became natural through its very continuation — gradually became spontaneous, and gushed forth from the depths of her soul. Her voice, quavering with emotion, became fainter and fainter, until it died away in an inarticulate moan.   Step by step she scaled the dangerous heights of religious ecstacy.

The baby, awakened by the noise and frightened by the strange face, began to cry and scream.

"Enough," shrieked the Doctor, angered at the interruption, dizzy from the motion, and weary of the din.

She fell to the earth with a shock that made every nerve in her body vibrate with pain and drew a long, deep groan from her lips.

"I will put this magic herb in this saucer," said the Doctor, taking a cracked china saucer from a shelf above the stove, "and set it out on the window ledge, so that the spirit of the Lord may rest upon it and bring its dead leaves to life again. And when the magic herb turns green then will your lover return, but not before then."

"Now to find the Quill and fix it up with him," he muttered to himself as he passed down the stairs, jingling the poor seamstress's coin in his pockets.

Twice that night did the Doctor's dupe arise to look at the magic herb to see if its color had changed to green, and twice she returned to her bed disappointed and in tears.

On the morrow she awoke with a thought of the plant, she sprang to the window and threw the shutters wide open; but still the same ball of dead brown met her anxious gaze.

Little basting did she do that day; between running to the window and talking to the baby of the good fortune that was to come, her time was spent.

Despite lightning, thunder and downpour of rain, she slept soundly through the succeeding night; for she was exhausted from loss of sleep and long-sustained excitement.

"It's green, it's green!" she cried joyfully, as with trembling hand she lifted the plant from the window ledge the next morning and kissed its green, shimmering fronds, sparkling with new-born life. "I knew that the good Lord would forgive my sin and answer my prayer."

Ann Garsch abandoned herself to happiness on that eventful day, and, daring the sweater's anger, entirely neglected her task;

in her eyes it would have been sacrilegious to have threaded a needle.

She tidied her room, washed and dressed the baby until he fairly shone from cleanliness; then she adorned herself with her best gown, and waited complacently for her lover.

The child laughed and lifted his chubby hands in a vain attempt to catch the sunbeams as they entered through the shutters and fell in prismatic splendor on his cradle; and the mother, finding the laughter infectious, joined him with a merry peal, and the baby redoubled its efforts on seeing her unusual gayety. Taking him in her arms, she began to dance around the room like a madcap, smothering her precious charge with kisses at every step.

The Quill entered at noon without preparing her for his coming by so much as a knock at the door; she fell into his arms, unable to speak from mere happiness, giving way to hysterical outbursts of tears and laughter.

When she had recovered from her aphony,

Ann blamed him in one breath for his baseness in deserting her, and blessed him in the next for the kindness of heart he displayed in returning.

He stood grinning stupidly through it all, receiving her commendation and blame alike impassively, as if considering his reception in the light of a joke.

The child was evidently not frightened by the stranger's face, he seemed willing enough to be taken when the mother held him out to the Quill; for he stretched his tiny arms fatherward, and looked his most enticing.

"Damn the brat," he said, turning away. The voice was so menacing that "the brat" began to cry with all his little might.

The Doctor, who was standing in the hallway, overheard what was going on inside, and thought if he wanted the remainder of his bill he had better make collections before the Quill succeeded in forcing his mistress to lament the advent of her lover.

She answered his knock, and gave him his

due without a murmur, dropping a blessing
with every coin that she let fall into his
itching palm.

The lover winked knowingly and grimaced
over the seamstress's shoulder at the Doctor.

"Who was that man? Why did you give
him that money?" he asked when the door
had shut.

In response she told the story of the
wonderful plant and the miracle it had
wrought.

"You do n't tell me," he whispered in
counterfeited awe; " I must have one of
'em."

Before she could stop him, the Quill was
darting down the stairs and into the street,
fearful lest his confederate had outdistanced
him and made away with the "swag."

While Ann Garsch stood at the doorway
with flushed cheeks and beating heart,
waiting for her lover to return, the Doctor
and the Quill almost came to blows at The
Lucky Number over the division of the
spoils.

The Return

ANGELO Pascella stepped into Rosaura Pascella's wine room and seating himself at one of his mother's tables, placed his carpet bag on the floor and called for *pranzo con mezza bottliglia di vino*, dinner with wine. The card-playing, eating, drinking, arguing Italians ceased their diversions long enough to take a look at the new comer.

He was a swarthy, healthy, prosperous looking fellow whose twenty-five years perched carelessly on his shoulders, as if perfectly willing to make room for a twenty-sixth. There was nothing in his looks, dress or manner that entitled him to a second glance, and no suspicion of vexing mystery arose in the minds of Rosaura's patrons to spoil the flavor of the *sphagetti importati*, or to interrupt the flow of wine and words and cards.

Madre Pascella, whose small shrewd eyes were boring through the stranger's carpet-sack to inventory the contents thereof, seeing a prospective patron in the stranger, hastened to wait on him herself, after soundly scolding the servant for not paying better attention to the wants of her customers,—this rather to impress the stranger than to reprove the servant.

Angelo, on his part, marvelled much at the little change that had taken place in his mother's appearance in the thirteen long years of his absence from home. She had grown somewhat stouter, the masculine growth on her upper lip was darker and thicker (those who spoke behind her back called it *un mostacchio*), her hair had lost its raven-like blackness, her face was a little more wrinkled, and that was all. Rosaura Pascella came of a stock that withers and dries, rather than dies.

The place, unlike its owner, was much the worse for wear; the plaster on the ceiling and walls was ready at any minute to fall on the floor, and seemed to beg for the support of props to prevent a tumble so disastrous. The floor had sagged under the heavy weight of the refrigerator and the clumsy pine bar; and both bar and refrigerator had arrived at that point of decrepitude where painting and repairing are too expensive to be practicable. The benches, tables and chairs — some minus an arm, some minus a leg, and some minus both — were the same ones around which Antonio had romped and played when a boy.

"Evidently the madre has not prospered since I left home; everything is going to rack and ruin," he reflected on looking around. Then, thinking of his own material success, "I shall put things to rights in less than no time."

When the mother placed the *pranzo* on the table, her son found it difficult to keep from throwing his arms around her, kissing her and crying, "*Mia carissima.*" But he held the reward of a more brilliant and sudden surprise before his eyes, and restrained himself.

He did not know whether to feel sad or

glad because she did not recognize him after an absence of only thirteen years. He knew her, forsooth! He gladdened himself with the reflection that he had outhandsomed her recollection, and ate on in silence, his eyes fixed on his plate. Ah! but the dish of spaghetti was fine, a motherly welcome in itself; and he smacked his lips and smiled contentedly. She was standing behind him with her arms folded, waiting for a chance to speak; she saw the smile and broke in abruptly, "How do you like it?"

"Fine," he answered, "just like my mother used to make," and he looked her straight in the eyes.

She bowed acknowledgment like one used to being complimented, and for whom one compliment is of as little value as another.

"I see," said she, pointing to the bag, "that you are from a distance."

"Yes, from New Orleans," — the words slipped from his lips inadvertently and he wished that he could recall them.

"Ehi! New Orleans!" The mere men-

tioning of the name changed her from an
inquisitive questioner into a most voluble
informer.   She had a son there in the fruit
business with her brother.   A fine lad, he
was, too!   He had left home when a boy of
twelve and had been gone thirteen years.
It was her only child; how she yearned to
see him again, her boy!   He might know
him, his name was Angelo Pascella?

Angelo shook his head.

"No?" she thought every Italian in New
Orleans must know her boy.   He had prospered, he was rich, he was influential.   He
had promised over and over again in his
letters to come home and spend a few days
with his old mother, but the years had gone
by and still he did not come.   Ah! if he
only knew the pleasure his return would
bring her, but young men were forgetful
and—

Someone at the farther end of the room
called for a bottle of wine, and her chatter
was interrupted.

Angelo looked through the room wistfully
to see if he could not discover some old

friends of his boyhood days. They were all gone, the old familiar faces, or, at least, none of them was there. A feeling of the transitoriness of things, of separation from the life of which he had once been a component part, touched him with a vague sense of loneliness. His coming home had made him home-sick, and he yearned to grasp his sack and start for New Orleans again. Then he blamed himself for not revealing his identity—a word from him and presto! all would change; his mother's arm would entwine lovingly about his neck, and his old friends would come crowding on the scene as if raised by magic. He would do it, surprise or no; but the sudden announcement ought to be surprise enough.

A diminutive, round-shouldered, bow-legged Italian entered the room and arrested Angelo's attention. He had seen a face like that somewhere, but he could not associate it with any particular place or time. But the legs? There was only one pair of legs in the world that bowed like those; surely enough, it must be little Pietro del Re, the tailor. Many an hour had he passed in the little tailor's basement shop, an ever welcome guest, listening to stories and descriptions of Italy and its wars.

He caught Pietro's eye and beckoned to him. "Would he have a glass of wine?" In a few minutes they were talking of the golden memories of the days gone by. Angelo felt his way carefully, and when the opportune moment came he discovered his identity. Pietro gave his head a jerk which made the rings in his ears dance. "What!" he exclaimed, "you do n't say, you—!"

The sentence was never finished save in the mind of the speaker, for Angelo clapped his hands over the mouth of the surprised tailor. "Hush!" whispered he, "I want to surprise her, and you will spoil it all." This mysterious action did not escape the attention of the madre, who was watching them from behind the bar.

"And you mean to say that she don't know you?" he jerked his thumb over his shoulder to designate the "she."

Angelo shook his head, "No, but I think I will tell her later, when the others are gone and we are left alone."

Pietro proposed a better scheme. Angelo's was not half dramatic enough to suit the imaginative tailor's conception of what a theatrical surprise should be. Angelo must go directly to bed; and he, Pietro, would immediately betake himself home. In the morning he would arise early and gather all the old friends, Cassaretto, Barretti, Salvino, De Stefano, and a host of others whom Angelo had known since his boyhood and about whom he had just been questioning Pietro. They would all assemble at the Osteria dell Gallo (the Inn of the Cock), and apprise the madre who her guest really was. Then she would rush upstairs, enter her son's room and have him wake in her arms; and when mother and son came down stairs the crowd would give them a rousing welcome.

"*Come vi piace?*" he asked.

Angelo rolled a cigarette, lit it, and thought awhile. "*Molto moltissimo*," he answered, blowing the cloud of thin smoke away.

The tailor shook hands, and arose for an immediate transaction of his part of the bargain.

At the doorway Rosaura stopped him — ''Who is the man, why did he put his hand over your mouth to prevent you from speaking?''

An imaginative mind is of service in more ways than one; Pietro manufactured a very plausible lie on the spur of the moment. ''He is a rich man, a very rich man, his pockets are lined with gold.   When he told me how much he had, 'What! so much as that!' I was about to cry, and up goes his hand over my mouth.   You see, Madre Pascello, he knows me to be an honest man; of the others he is not so sure.   Good night.''

Rosaura was still reflecting on how much truth there might be in the tailor's lie when Angelo approached and asked to be shown to his room.   Here was an opportunity to make this stranger show the material with which his pockets were lined, and to prove him a Crœsus, or Pietro del Re a liar.

"The rules of the house are to pay in advance,"she said authoritatively, her hands on her hips.

The stranger smiled quietly, drew a fat roll of bills from the inside pocket of his vest and paid the amount demanded in a way that said, "And I would n't care if it were a little higher."

The sight of it made her eyes ache and the palms of her hands itch. There was more than enough in that one roll to pay her year's rent, and in the morning Carlo Neppi, the landlord, would be around clamoring for his money; and Neppi was terrible when the rent was not ready, all counted out in dimes and quarters and dollar bills — he would throw her into the streets, and give her a shrug of his shoulders for sympathy.

She lit a kerosene lamp, and opened the door that shut the saloon from the winding stairway which led to the lodging-house above. As they were moving down the narrow hall-way towards the room designated for Angelo, he gave way to a sudden impulse, caught her round her ample waist and kissed her. "Go away, fool!" she cried, shoving him vigorously against the wall. She entered the room, put the lamp on the washstand, and made her exit without even wishing him good night.

It was the room he had occupied when a boy; the wash-stand, the bed, the stool, all looked as if they had been waiting for him, and a Murillo Madonna, a cheap, dust-mellowed lithograph, beamed a welcome home from her place on the wall. There was little enough in that bare room about which old memories could cluster; but they clung all the more closely to the small space available, like vines that put forth their creepers to mass their foliage about a single nail in an old wall.

Just below his window, which looked on the street, the signboard (a cock with the inscription "Osteria dell Gallo") was creaking loudly as it swayed back and forth in the wind. Angelo regulated the creaking to the refrain, "wel-come home, wel-come home,'' and his imagination made the inanimate cock crow the words softly. The refrain soon lulled him to sleep.

Downstairs Rosaura was bubbling over with impatience; it seemed to her that midnight, the hour for closing, would never come, and that the loiterers would never go.

"It is past twelve; come, pay; it is very late, I must close or disobey the ordinance," she said to Enrico Grassi, who was telling her for the tenth time how Paolo Cherino had cheated him out of the last game of *morra*, and how Paolo, and not he, should pay for the last drinks.

"In a minute, just a minute, and I have done," repeated the excited Enrico. "When a man has only a half thumb and bends it half-way, it would take the devil himself to tell whether it was up or down. 'Four,' says I! 'Three,' says Paolo, 'you pay.' Now Madre, I leave it to you if—"

"I care not whether it was up or down, Paolo has gone and you must pay!" cried the bored and impatient hostess.

"Well," said Enrico, with a shrewd smile,

"you are like the rest of them, you are in the conspiracy to cheat me. Charge it!" and out he went with a slam of the door.

"It was worth the price of two glasses of wine to be rid of the fellow," she reflected philosophically, as she locked the door and turned the lamps out.

She moved up the stairs as carefully as if each inch of the way were connected by wire with bells, and the slightest jar would start the bells ringing and awaken some restless sleeper.

When in her room she removed her shoes and walked cautiously, on tip-toe, to the door that divided Angelo's room from her own, and pressed her ear against it. She heard the sleeper's deep and regular breathing, significant of one who has a light heart and an easy conscience for bed fellows. "He sleeps too soundly," she thought, "for a man with so much money."

She drew the bolt quietly, bent her knee against the panel of the door, waited a second in breathless suspense; then pressed forward quickly and turned the knob; the door opened as noiselessly as if the hinges had been oiled.

His bed was just opposite the door, and she could see every line of his youthful face by the light cast from the lamp that she had left burning low on a chair in the center of her own room.

She advanced to his bedside slowly, slowly; the distance was but a few feet; to her it seemed as many miles. He had his vest buttoned over his woolen night-gown; it was the object of her search, and she noticed it before anything else. She bent over him, so closely that she could feel the moisture of his breath on her hot cheek.

As Rosaura stood thus, holding her sti-letto in her right hand, and firmly and gent-ly unbuttoning his vest with her left hand, it seemed to her that she had seen the man before. So forcibly did the idea strike her that she paused in the very heat and excite-ment of the action to scan the sleeper's fea-tures more closely.

He turned on his side as if troubled by

her searching stare and buried his face in the pillow.

She raised her stiletto, ready to strike if he awoke. His breathing continued regular and rounded as the ticking of an oscillating pendulum.

Then with one quick movement of the stiletto she ripped his vest down the back, and the heavier half of the garment, the half with the purse, she removed by a single tug.

In an over-anxiety to secure her treasure without awakening him, she let the stiletto slip and it pricked him in the back. He awoke with a start. Fearful lest he cry aloud, she grasped him by the throat with her long, knotty, masculine fingers, and the battle began for supremacy between mother and son.

The son was the stronger, but the mother had all the advantages of position, forewarning and forearming. He used his strong arms for levers and tried to raise his body to a sitting posture. Her grasp tightened, and he felt the life-breath being choked out of him as she forced him on his back. He swung his left arm out in a half circle and struck her a staggering blow on the temple; she reeled, stretched out her long arm and caught the bed-post to save herself from falling.

Angelo sprang to his feet, and was on the floor in almost the time it took Rosaura's arm to reach out and grasp for support. He recognized his assailant and stood terror-stricken, dumb-founded, paralyzed, "*Madre mia, madre mia!*" he gasped plaintively, beseechingly. The stiletto was drawn back, flashed, and leaped straight to his heart.

She crept on her hands and knees to the hall door, opened it and listened. The living were as silent as the murdered; the dead and the sleeping could tell no tales.

Pietro's sleep was by no means as sound as that of Angelo's. He tossed about restlessly the whole night, laying his plan of attack for the great surprise on the morrow; for Pietro was a simple soul who made the most of one of those rare opportunities that gave him half a chance to appear of importance in the community.

He had made his plans a score of times, and changed them just as often; he would go for Antonio Salvino first and have him summon Gustavo de Stefano, and Gustavo and Antonio could summon those who lived south of the Osteria; whilst he, himself, could gather those who lived in another direction. No, he would go first to Gaetano Negrini's, that would save time, for although Gaetano lived a little farther away, he was much the younger man and could move much the quicker. To have them assemble there together at seven o'clock to the minute, that was a task which would require skillful manœuvering! Rather than be one minute late, Pietro preferred being three hours ahead of time, and the dawn had preceded him only by a few minutes when he made his way towards Negrini's domicile.

As he passed the Osteria he was surprised beyond measure to see Rosaura assisting two burly, desperate appearing Italians (entire strangers to Pietro) to shove a long pine box on a rickety express-wagon.

"Something always goes wrong," he growled, "I wonder what business she has to nose about at this hour! Something to do with Angelo, I'll wager. She always finds out everything, the Madre."

"A distinguished looking visitor we had last night," he began tentatively.

She was so surprised to see him there that she almost let her end of the box fall.

"Oh, it's you, is it, Pietro? And what are you doing around at this time of day?" She shouted some unnecessary directions to the assistants to hide her discomposure.

"I was about to ask the same question of you," answered Pietro guardedly.

"That's my affair," she retorted sharply.

The timid tailor stood abashed and for want of something better to relieve his embarrassment, he repeated abstractedly, "A distinguished looking visitor we had last night."

She flushed perceptibly and relaxed her

hold on the box. "Take care!" cried one of the men.

"What visitor?" She shifted her position so that her back was turned to the interrogator.

"Why, the young man, the good looking chap with the carpet-bag."

"Oh, he—how should I know who he was? He went away last night." Her dark face flushed again and she felt the blood beat at her temples; she blest her good sense for having turned her back to his face.

At last the box was on the wagon, and the two desperados jumped on the seat and drove rapidly towards the south.

"Gone away! A nice trick to serve me! All my pains for nothing. I wonder if she tells the truth?" he muttered.

Rosaura stood on the edge of the curb watching the wagon until it passed from sight, then she turned towards the house. Pietro stood thinking what tactics he would employ to gain the truth.

"You there yet?" she said, turning around, "I thought you had gone long ago."

"I—I am not sure whether I understand," answered Pietro, apologetically. "Did you say he went away?"

"Of course I said so. Have you grown deaf; do you want me to repeat it a dozen times?" She was again the master of her expression, or rather of her inexpression.

"Did he tell you where he was going? Did he leave his name? Did he tell you when he would return?"

"Why should he tell me such things, what am I to him? I gave him his lodging and he paid me; there our business ended."

"But, Madre Pascella, I know who he was; I'll give you ten guesses, and if you guess right, I will treat to a bottle of your best, when he returns; and if you don't guess the treat is yours. Come, now," said Pietro in one breath anxious to surprise Rosaura and have a part of his glory at least, since the full measure had been denied him.

The blood left her dark cheeks and she blanched visibly. Had he suspected something? Was he trying to bulldoze her into a confession and hush-money? She would show him with what kind of a *man* he was dealing.

"Guess, guess! Do you think I have nothing better to do than to stand here on the sidewalk and waste my precious time guessing with an old fool when I have breakfast to get for twenty?" She pushed him to one side and started towards the door.

The awed tailor (it takes nine tailors to make a man, the world over), fearing lest some one else, waiting inside with the surprise all ready, might cheat him out of his hard-earned reward, and seeing his dream. of glory fade into nothingness, hastened to say: "Madre Pascella, it was your son Angelo, he told me so last night in the wine room. That's why he put his hand over my mouth. 'Angelo, you!' I was about to cry. 'Hush, you fool,' says he, and up goes his hand over my mouth. Yes, it was Angelo, and I alone am in the secret; in me alone—"

"*Dio del Cielo!*" cried Rosaura, and fell swooning to the ground.

The Flight of a Night-hawk

"She loves flowers and she's unmarried. What luck!"
—BALZAC.

"PIDGY" Donnavan pitched his night-hawk just around the corner from The Lucky Number, threw a heavy blanket over the flanks of his shivering horse, and, rubbing his nostrils caressingly, said; "It's freezin' cold, Major, an' hard pullin', but there 'll be heavy graft for us to-night, or I'll be disappinted."

Pidgy — short for Pigeon, shorter still for Pigeon-toed, — his night-hawk, and Major, were well known in the neighborhood, for they had helped more than one thief elude the police, and had played their parts (they were often cast for the chief rôles in the play) in more than one daring robbery.

I said "they," because the play could no more go on without Major and the night-hawk than it could without Pidgy himself.

124

They were the three legs of a tripod, remove one, and crash! the whole comes tumbling to the ground.   Two of the legs of this tripod must certainly have been born for each other; the third I know was made to suit the other two.   Pidgy and Major were born to illustrate the proverb that appearances are deceitful,—a proverb which ever needs new illustrations,—and to prove it the night-hawk was manufactured.   Pidgy expressed the quality of stupidity envisaged; Major that of slowness; and the night-hawk that of clumsiness;—but the rickety, ramschackle night-hawk could roll over the ground noiselessly and swiftly as a rubber ball down an inclined plane; Major's long bony body could fly along like a hare before the hounds; Pidgy, cunning, alert, shrewd, could change the expression of stupidity on his face as easily as the glove on his hand.

However, on this night they had no intention of violating the law; they were there for an entirely different purpose; their intention was to catch a thief, and not to assist one to escape.

Right in the doorway of The Lucky Number stood the man wanted by them and the police; Pidgy had seen him there but a few minutes ago, and he had good reason to believe that he was still there.

The police had offered a reward of eight hundred dollars for his arrest and conviction, and Pidgy was anxious to catch "the bird," not so much for the reward, although that was by no means to be despised, as for the pleasure of seeing "the bird" confined behind the bars of an iron cage from which there was no escape.

Three hours had not passed since the captain of the station had told him that Joe Coombs, *alias* "the Gold Brick," was wanted by the police, and wanted so badly that they would cheerfully pay the sum of eight hundred dollars for his capture. The captain knew if any man could find him it was Pidgy, and, furthermore, he knew that there were reasons other than the reward which would act like a spur in the chase.

"I dunno," said Pidgy to the captain, as he opened his broad mouth on the bias, and grinned stupidly, and peered rather than looked at him with his small, dull grey eyes, "I dunno," but Pidgy did know.

No sooner did he leave the captain than he began to search for Kate, the flower girl. To find Kate when looking for Joe is as good as finding one end of a rope when you want the other; it is only a question of time before you have both. Kate and Joe were ardent and inseparable lovers, and Pidgy, loving Kate with an ardor and fervor equal to Joe's, hated Joe as intensely as he loved Kate.

Pidgy's vitals were being consumed by a fire of jealousy, for he could never understand why Kate should prefer "a gun"* and "prowler" to a cab driver of his acknowledged ability; and the harder he tried to solve the problem the more difficult did it seem, and the more vexed and angry did Pidgy become. "It's them large puppy-dog eyes of hisn," he would conclude after giving the problem up in confusion. "I'd like to jerk 'em out of his nut, I would."

*Daring thief.

Joe had every advantage over him in all the qualities of appearance and manner that go towards making a man attractive to a woman; but Pidgy had the advantage of quantity, of mere brute bulk and force, and he would have used it more than once with telling effect had not Kate interfered.

In the charm of her presence and against her coquetry and tact, Pidgy's strength counted as naught; she could move him as easily as she could twirl her flower-tray around her little finger. Once she coaxed money from him for the purpose, candidly avowed, of paying Joe's fine; nor did she have to coax so very hard either — simply a demure little kiss, a slight pressure of his hand, and Pidgy drew out his leather bag and handed her the money. But when Kate and the money were gone, he cursed himself for a born fool, and kicked the walls of his stable in a fit of jealousy and rage; and then he calmed himself by reflecting that she would have hoodwinked Joe out of money for a like purpose in his behalf. Then he threw himself into a towering rage again by reflecting that she could n't and she would n't.

Even a cab driver may hitch his wagon, if not his cab, to a star and long for the unattainable, and the more Kate neglected Pidgy and showed favor to Joe, by so much the more did Pidgy long for Kate. Moreover, he laid great stress on the priority of his acquaintanceship, and trusted that it would count for much in his favor when the battle was finally decided. Pidgy had known Kate from the first days of her teens, and had watched with fearful heart this tender blossom on the tree of life, exposed as it was to such rough winds and weather, expand slowly and wonderfully into well-rounded completeness. Long before Joe had ever known or seen her, Pidgy had rendered the girl many a small service, and some large ones, too, for the matter of that; and on this account Kate could never bring herself to sever the delicate cords of sentiment and friendship and love that held them together.

So Pidgy loved on with a hope at which

hope itself mocked, purely, courageously; and the purity and courageousness of his love were worthy of a cavalier in the days of chivalry, for in love and in death—the two powers by which God asserts man's equality —are not all men equal?

Because Kate could love a thief like Joe you may have a poor opinion of her. You have already, no doubt, preconceived that she was all a woman ought not to be; such a preconception, if tranquillizing to the proprieties, is shocking to the truth, and it must, therefore, be challenged.

Kate was reared in an atmosphere of crime and sin, she had seen their terrible results, and she had been warned time and time again by the victims to pay no heed to their wiles and blandishments. She passed through the foul atmosphere untainted and unstained. An object lesson is worth all the text lessons in the world, and Kate had learned that virtue was its own reward; and the use of her eyes, without the slightest aid from her reason, forced her to the conclusion.

For eight years and over she had contributed an unequal share towards the support of a worthless family by peddling flowers. With her little tray of assorted roses and carnations, she had passed day in, day out, over disreputable thresholds and from saloon to saloon; and the end of her twentieth year found her as pure and blameless in the sight of God as she was at the beginning of her twelfth.

In the swamps of Florida there grows the tulip orchid—"a learned man could give it a clumsy name"—of the most exquisite pink shade and the most delicate shape; and this flower hangs pendant upon its stem, and dreams, like Heine's palm, of purer worlds, as it sways to and fro in that pestilential, miasmatic air. In Kate human nature had produced such an anomaly.

While Pidgy was driving along leisurely towards Kate's home after leaving the captain, he caught sight of Joe in the doorway of The Lucky Number. Pidgy was not surprised to see him, he half expected it; for Joe and Kate usually met there, and from

the logic of experience he deduced the conclusion that they had appointed that particular spot to meet each other on this night.
The police could easily have been warned
and Joe captured then and there, but
Pidgy had two good reasons for not inform-
ing on him; first, the police would probably
claim the whole reward for themselves; and
second, he would cheat himself out of the
vengeance for which he thirsted. He wanted
"the Gold Brick" to know — and he hoped
the knowledge would torture him to death
slowly,—that it was Pidgy Donnavan's power
and skillful manœuvering that had landed
him behind the bars.

When Pidgy pitched his cab on the corner
near The Lucky Number, he had resolved
upon an audacious adventure; and in
the dense darkness he waited impatiently for
things to reach the point that would admit
of his assistance in their development.

Meanwhile "the Gold Brick" was growing anxious and restless, and he found it
difficult to remain at the tryst; for not long
before he had heard from a friend, who was

on the inside and had "a pull," that he was wanted at the station, and wanted eight hundred dollars' worth.

He thought that the world was unjust, and that the police, who ran it, would turn paradise into a botch; because he had not been at all concerned in the daring and successful robbery for which they were holding him responsible, and in fact no one was more surprised than he to hear the story of its execution.

But that was neither here nor there; he was wanted and if the police found him, it was an easy matter "to fix" their scales, and find him wanting.

There was but one thing to do; to leave town, and leave quickly. His train started at nine and he was ready to go, ticket and baggage were in his pocket; but he dared not go without saying good-bye to Kate.

Unfortunately, he had made the appointment with her on the night before, and to leave so suddenly and without any explanation might offend her egregiously, and smooth the way, heretofore stony and rough enough, for the entrance of his persistent and ubiquitous rival.

She had promised to be there at half past eight, and it was now twenty minutes to nine, and she was nowhere in sight.

The cold was growing sharper and more penetrating with every minute, and Joe's patience waned as the cold waxed. The snow, that had fallen steadily during the day, was being swirled into wave-shaped drifts and piles; so the street had the appearance of a great heaving ocean of clear white; and, as if to perfect the resemblance, this same wind-sprite was gathering huge handfuls of the snow, grinding it into powder and blowing it about like so much ocean-spray.

Joe jumped up and down, first on one foot, then on the other, and threw his arms vigorously across his chest to keep the sluggish current of his blood from stagnation, and his patience, slowly sinking, from death. He gazed anxiously, nervously, down the long vista of the street, and still no Kate.

The chances of catching his train were reduced by another five minutes, when he, reflecting that there was a slight possibility of reaching the station in time by the aid of a cab, saw the tall robust figure of Kate, clad in a long black coat, hurriedly making its way up the street. The flickering light of the street-lamps made her form stand out in silhouette-like relief against the background of dazzling white.

He raised the collar of his ulster and, holding the ends of it over his face, hastened forward. They mét where one end of the short dark alley that bisects the block loses its identity in the main street.

"Ther ain't no time left for billin' and cooin' around, Kate," remarked Joe, after blurting out what had happened.

"Cab, sir," bawled Pidgy, through his thick heavy scarf, as he drove towards them leisurely.

"Yes, hold on!" called Joe. He drew Kate to him, kissed her passionately, and jumped into Pidgy's night-hawk.

"Good-bye! Good luck!" called Kate.

"I love you, I love you, I will always love you!"

"Make my train and there's a V for you;" Joe slammed the door and the cab started.

To Pidgy, Kate's adieu sounded like the falling melancholy notes of a funeral march for the dead love that had lived and yearned in his heart but a minute ago. He clenched his teeth firmly, swung his craft northwards, and started on at full speed. The bird had hopped right into the trap, and had taken the precaution of locking itself in; if the bird "ducked" it would be the fault of the trap, and not of the sportsman.

The jail was on the way to the railway station, and just a few blocks to the east; he had only to stop his cab there, throw the door open, grab his bird by the throat, call to the police, claim his reward, and laugh right in the bird's face. When the bird was in the "stir"* and the eight hundred dollars in his pockets, he could start a livery, marry Kate, and thus see the two great ambitions

*Penitentiary.

of his life accomplished,—the one great ambition, I might say, for the one was but the
complement of the other.

The depressing music of the funeral
march that her adieu had awakened in his
heart died away before the stirring, inspirit-
ing notes of a march of triumph.

"Go it, Major, go it!" and Pidgy's whip
came down on his back with a crash. A
whip was seldom if ever used on Major, for
it was seldom needed; but when the lash
snapped Major knew that the occasion was
extraordinary, and he struck his best pace.
The cab sped over the ground as if Major
were laboring under the delusion that he was
attached to a sulky and trotting on a race
track.

Several times he thought that he heard
the sound of carriage wheels breaking
through the crisp snow close behind him; he
turned on his box to peer through the darkness. He could discover nothing, but he
still heard the sound, and his fancy coined
the superstition that he was running a race
with a phantom cab whose wraith of a

driver was trying to upset him, and seize his prize.

Pidgy intended that no driver real or imaginary should catch up to him, and he made his horse speed through the snow as the poor beast never sped through it before.

Major was crossing a corner at break-neck speed, when Pidgy jerked him back on his haunches with a suddenness that almost rolled the night-hawk into the snow. "W-h-o-a, Major, w-h-o-a!" he called hoarsely.

In heaven's name, what manner of cab was that whose horse had passed through his night-hawk with the speed of the wind, and, like the wind, left no rack or ruin behind? And what manner of person was that seated within, and looking for all the world like Kate?

"Ye're got 'em again, man, and without drink," Pidgy whispered to himself, wiping the cold sweat from his brow. If a cab run through yer cab, it ud bust it clean; and if it did run through yer cab and not bust it, it wan't no cab, no nothing. And as fer

Kate bein' in that cab, how could Kate be in the cab, if it wan't no cab?'' Thus did Pidgy argue his fancy out of the illusion of a phantom cab.

Now, four blocks more to the right, and they would be at the jail. He turned down the dark side street, his hand trembling so violently that he could scarcely keep a tight rein.

Another block and he could pull his cab up in front of the broad, stone stairs of the ''boobyhatch;'' already he could descry through the darkness its somber gray walls.

Pidgy gave an involuntary shudder; he had been behind those walls himself, and knowing how gray and blank and desolate they were, he preferred the darkness and the cold of the outer world a thousand times.

A phantasmagorial hand was trying to jerk the lines from his grasp and pull Major back on his reckless course; and right in front of him, so near that its lips almost touched his own, was a face, ghostly white, whiter than the snow that glistened on the roof of the jail—the hand and the face were

Kate's. The lips of that face opened and moaned beseechingly, "For God's sake do n't take him there, anywhere but there! I'll kill myself if you do! I love him; I love him; I will always love him!"

That it was a figment of the imagination Pidgy knew then, just as well as he knows it to-day; but for a moment the illusion was real and vivid and horrible enough. He knew, too, that the voice which came from those lips was only the voice of his own conscience, but it was sepulchral and terrifying for all of that.

"No, by God, I'll not!" he muttered. " The girl loves him and I loves the girl, let the girl have him! Damn his puppy-dog eyes anyway!" He swung his cab on past the jail, and veering in another direction, made for the station.

Whether it was from the battle of conflicting emotions or the intense excitement, or the excessive jolting and rocking, the fact is Pidgy grew dizzy; and it seemed to him that his cab stood still and the ground glided and slipped from under Major's hoofs.

Joe was wondering why the man turned corners so often, but it was too dark to tell where they were going and he thought the cabby must surely know.

It was just three minutes to nine when the poor, wind-broken, foam-covered animal stopped in front of the depot. Joe flung down the fare, and darted for his train.

"And neither of 'em 'ell never know it, Major," muttered Pidgy, as he gulped down a big lump in his throat and ploughed homeward through the pitiless darkness of the night.

A Fair Exchange

"What entered into thee
That was, is and shall be."
—BROWNING.

PART I.

AN OLD HYPOTHESIS.

THE air of wealth and luxury that hovered about the nurse and the baby she carried would have told you at a glance that they did not belong in the tenement district through which they were passing. The expensive linen of the baby, and the nurse's long gray cloak and Alsatian cap, with its fluttering blue ribbons, stood out as boldly in relief from the squalor of that poverty-stricken district as a box of flaring red geraniums from the soot blackness of a tenement window frame.

Nevertheless, the girl carried the baby into one of those tumble-down residences of the poor, and up the winding flight of greasy, worn stairs. When she had left the last stairs of the fourth flight behind, she walked down the narrow hall, and knocked at the first door at her left.

An unkempt woman, bent, flat-chested and thin-featured, opened the door.

"Oh, it's you, Mag, is it? Come in."

On the carpetless floor of the room that the girl entered three babies were playing and crying; or, to be more explicit, two were crying, and one was playing.

"How's the kids, ma?" asked Mag.

Ma shrugged her stoop shoulders, and pointed with her hand to the articles in question in a way that said, "They 're there, see fer yourself; what does yer care anyway."

The hands and shoulders were in the right, for the daughter thought the mere question displayed sufficient interest in the younger members of the family, and she paid no further attention to them.

The atmosphere was stifling, choking. The June sun poured its molten heat through the broken glass panes of the low windows with a remorseless, savage energy; the squat ceiling and the paperless walls, from which the plaster was dropping in large squares and oblongs, seemed to vie with each other in their greed to catch every sun ray that entered. From the next room, kitchen, laundry, and living apartment, all in one, there came floating in a swarm of oppressive odors, strongly suggestive of the frying pan.

"What brings yer here again, Mag?" asked the mother after they had sat through a minute's embarrassing silence.

"I'm going to run out to the grocery-man's picnic for the rest of the afternoon, and I thought as you'd mind the kid for me."

Without waiting for a reply the girl doffed her gown and cap, and laid them on the trundle bed carefully. Then, in a manner that showed she had done the same thing before, she divested her charge of its fine linen, and dressed it in a garment of cheap, coarse material, brought with her for the purpose. As she undressed him—for it was a boy — the delightful fragrance of violet perfume was perceptible for the second or two before it was suffocated in a struggle for survival.

The unrobing and robing done, she placed the baby on the floor to amuse himself as best he could, which was not very well, for the child of luxury rebelled against the plebeian surroundings, and he sent up an agonizing howl every time the proletarian children touched the hem of his skirts.

The mother grumbled about extra work, an ungrateful daughter, and the brats of the rich.

"Here, take this," and Mag handed her a silver dollar; having expected it, she was prepared to overcome the grumbling.

"It's all I could save this week."

"She comes handy," said the woman rolling the dollar in a rag of a handkerchief, and slipping it back into her rag of a gown. "The old man's been out of work all week, and ain't brought home a red. You're a good gurl, Mag, I allus said it! Ain't you got another 'roller' fer yer ma?"

"How's the old man," asked the girl evasively.

"Find and ask him," replied the mother, "he's rolling around drunk somewhere's; ain't seen 'im fer two days."

"Now, Harvey R. Garwood, Jr., you be good while I'm gone or"—and Mag shook her fist at the child from the doorway as a parting admonition, and left for the picnic. The child yelled and screamed with all the power of his little lungs, for he was finding his strange companions and abiding place more and more loathsome; and when his nurse disappeared he felt like a ship-captain who sees his mutinous crew sail out on the open seas, far away from the deserted island where the wretches have left him to die.

At five o'clock Mag returned to the tenement, her cheeks deeply flushed, and her breath smelling of whiskey. She laughed hilariously as she gave her mother an incoherent, but highly-colored account of the picnic; and the mother laughed just as hilariously, and the comments with which she interspersed Mag's narrative were just as incoherent as the narrative itself. She had spent her dollar at The Lucky Number for the same good cheer that Mag had found at the picnic.

The girl hastened to prepare her charge for the return homeward. "Hold on, Mag, hold on," hiccoughed the mother. "I got a scheme for both en us; bin thinkin' on it all afternoon. Why can't us let our kid be brung up among the swell uns, eh? What's wrong with my kid doddin' round in silk and livin' swell, I wants ter know? What's the difference twixt my kid and their kid?"

She shrieked with laughter, and then cried her eyes red with maudlin tears; when the tears ceased and the laughter subsided, she explained her scheme: she fancied that there was a strong resemblance between her youngest son and her daughter's charge. Why not change them? Why not let her boy grow up rich and well tended, and the rich boy wear rags? When he grew to a man's estate he would reward them richly for the clever ruse they had played for his benefit.

This, in brief, was the plan that the whiskey had inspired in her heated imagination, and which she proceeded to give in detail and with much circumlocution and many bitter invectives against the rich, who were cheating them at every turn and crook of the long road of life.

Mag was just drunk enough to consent to such a wild undertaking; the whiskey in her case, as in her mother's, had exaggerated the faint resemblance of the children into a positive likeness, and she swore the one might easily be made to do service for the other.

So the pauper went to the palace, and the prince remained in the slums.

PART II.

ENVIRONMENT—A PROBABILITY.

At the rear of The Lucky Number, under a hollow made by the framework of the outside stairway, is a heap of old rags collected by " The Kid," and used by him for a "doss."*

*Bed.

What the origin of "The Kid" was no one knew, he did not even know himself; he had slept there as far back as the oldest patron of the place could remember, and beyond that there was nothing known of him; but who cared one way or the other?

"The Kid's" antics were amusing, and he was in no one's way; in fact, he proved a positive attraction to the place, and he was allowed to remain there unmolested. It afforded the hobos infinite amusement to see the little fellow drain a can of beer, smoke a pipe of strong tobacco, sing vile songs, and tell still viler stories. Had a full-fledged hobo told the same stories or sang the same songs, they would have fallen flat, but done by "The Kid" they had a zest and drollery which provoked delirious laughter and rounds of applause. "He's knowin', dat 'smooth';* he's wise as 'a jocker',† they would say as they winked slyly and poked one another in the ribs.

*Young thief.
†Old thief, one with whiskers.

The lore of things forbidden was as an open book to him, for he had the most able teachers in the world, and he was a particularly brilliant pupil; often the masters quarreled among themselves for the honor of having taught him in this or that branch in which he excelled.

Such surroundings and such influences had moulded his exterior just as ductile metal is shaped by the rigid form of the mould into which it is poured. He could not have been over ten years of age, but his growth had been so stunted by the beer and the tobacco that he was no taller than the average healthy boy of eight. His thin chest, and thinner body, his hollow cheeks and sallow complexion—sallow to the point of greenness—bespoke a poorly nourished and morbid condition of the tissues.

Had he stuck his head through a canvas and exposed his face only to view, it would have puzzled you to have guessed his age. The lines of his face were hard and set, its expression was that of an habitual criminal grown old in vice, and yet the features were

those of a mere boy in the formative period
of life. But the crux of the difficult puzzle
was the eyes; he had the most serene, innocent brown eyes it was ever your pleasure
to look into, and with those innocent eyes he
could look you straight in the face and tell
lies by the score.

One day, while going on an errand for
Mike, the bartender, he lost his way, an
unusual thing for him to do; and while wandering about he stumbled into the most im-
posing residence street of the city. "The
Kid" had never been there before; indeed
it was one of his first trips beyond the
limits of the slums. He had no more occasion for going into this residence district of
the wealthy than a child of a millionaire has
for going into the slums.

"Gawd!" he exclaimed, "but this is dead
swell," and he sat on a brown stone coping
to take it in slowly.

"Hi, you there, get off that fence!"
yelled a man from the yard, "I just cleaned
it!"

"The Kid" put his right hand to his

nose and jumped; the action was so comical that the man laughed aloud.　His laughter aroused the urchin's anger, "I'd like ter have him alone by De Lucky Number," he muttered.

A boy with long golden curls, and dressed *à la* Fauntleroy was riding down the street on a velocipede.

"Hello!" cried the boy.

"Howdy!" answered "The Kid."

"My name is Harvey R. Garwood, Jr.; what's yours?"

He was about to answer that he was called "The Kid," but it sounded like nothing in comparison with the long, aristocratic roll of Harvey R. Garwood, Jr., so he checked himself and said simply, "I ain't got none!"

"That's funny," laughed the other; "my mamma says everybody has a name."

"Well, yer ma don't know it all.　I knows lots of folks what ain't got no names."　And he spat straight for an elm tree, some eight or ten feet off, and hit it squarely.

"That's great," shouted Lord Fauntle-roy, "do it again."

The Arab spat again with equal precision.

"Now let me try it," and the Lord tried until the roof of his mouth became dry and parched.

"Say, but yer green," said "The Kid," with a look of infinite disparagement.

Anxious to show his other accomplishments he played drunk and rolled and staggered about on the grass like an old intoxicant; Harvey laughed until the tears rolled down his cheeks.

"Maybe you'd like to ride on my velocipede? I can ride it all over. Do you know how to ride?"

"Fer sure I do," he had never been on one in his life, but there was nothing "The Kid" was afraid to try, and he rode away as if he had come into the world on a wheel. He liked the exercise so well that his first intention was to run away with the velocipede, but he wanted to hear "de swell guy" praise his cleverness, so he turned around and rode back, trusting to luck to make away with it afterwards.

He found "de swell guy" in a flood of tears, crying as though his heart would break.

"What is yer spilling 'bout, I did n't hurt de ding?

"I lost my new knife with the pearl handle and four blades. I l-o-s-t it!" he boohooed.

"The Kid" grinned, " Here it be," and he handed the knife to him with an air made up of amusement and superiority.

"Where did you find it? I looked all over for it," and his face changed from grave to gay with child-like rapidity.

" I dlipped it from yer prat-kick."*

"Where did you find it? I did n't understand where you said?"

"Say, but yer green. I means I took her from yer back pocket," answered the rogue blandly.

*Britch is used to designate the front-pocket; gerve, vest-pocket; insider, inside coat-pocket; fob, small side coat-pocket; smoker, any pocket in which a pocket-book (skin) happens to be.

"From my pocket?"

"Yop!"

"But I did n't feel you take it," and his eyes opened wide as saucers.

"Say, but yer easy. Dat's de game; course yer did n't feel it!"

"If you show me the trick, I'll let you ride my wheel again."

"Naw, yer kin never learn it, it takes too long ter ketch onto de spiel."

He put the knife way down in the depths of his velvet trousers, and held his hand over it to make sure that the magician should n't conjure the recovered treasure away again.

The magician started to sing "Dad Dooley's Daughter," and Garwood, Jr. liked the ditty so well that he begged him to continue, remarking, "That's awfully funny; I wish I could learn it."

"I 'll learn yer, it goes like dis," and he hummed: —

> " Dad Dooley had a daughter
> What was hot in love wid me,
> Till a sailor laddy caught her,
> And dey runned across de sea.

"O Dad Dooley's puttee daughter,
Oh, yer broke me heart yer did,
When yer skipped across de water
Wid de jolly sailor kid."

The prince proved a poor scholar; he forgot the first line as soon as he had learned the second, and the pauper gave his pupil up in disgust.

"I learned dat song de fust crack; I'm smarter en you."

"No you ain't! I go to school, and I'm in the third reader, and I'm the best reader in the class."

"I don't care ef yer in de leventh reader, I'm smarter en you."

"No you're not."

"Yes I be."

How long the dispute might have continued in this strain there is no telling, had not the aristocrat missing his knife, started to cry. The Arab returned it without comment, but with an air that was deliciously droll.

"I'll whip you if you take my knife again," and the lace ruffles were rolled back from the wrist.

"Come, what's de use ef scrappin', life's too short;"—this was a favorite quotation used at The Lucky Number before and after a fight as a kind of sedative, which "The Kid" had swallowed without knowing its nature. A feeling of love and companionship for the little stranger who had treated him kindly stirred the lad to the depths of his being, and he put his arms around the stranger's neck affectionately.

He pushed him away, "Your hand's all dirt, and you'll dirty my waist, and I put it on clean this morning."

"Dat's nuffin, de dirt 'ell come off. Look at me," and it dawned upon his quick intelligence that a great, yawning abyss lay between him and the young aristocrat.

The prince was just as quick to note the change of expression on the other's face. "Don't feel bad, I've got some old ones in the linen closet and I'll give them to you;" after a pause, "you must be very poor, and my mamma says I must be good to the poor. My papa's rich, and he owns a large factory with big chimneys; it's lots of fun to watch the smoke. He buys me everything, my papa.''

Now "The Kid" understood the real significance of the words rich and poor; now, too, he caught a glimmering, vague as it was, of the meaning of the wild harangues delivered at The Lucky Number in which the grinding rich were anathematized and the suffering poor canonized.

He was busy uniting the scattered sixes and sevens of his brain into thirteens when the boy interrupted, "I'm hungry, I'm going into the house to get something to eat, come ahead. Does your mamma allow you to eat between meals?''

The pauper stood lost in amazement. He was going to explain that, in the first place, he was glad to pick up a crumb at any time, between, or at the ends; and, in the second place, that he had no mamma to regulate the time when he might stoop to gather the crumbs; but, not wishing the other's superiority to shine forth too glaringly, he answered indifferently, "Sometimes she do, and sometimes she do n't.''

They met no menial at the palace gate to challenge the entrance of the stranger, and the two made their way undisturbed and without difficulty into the banquet hall of the king.

The pauper was bewildered; he had never dreamt that anything so marvelous or enchanting as that banquet hall existed anywhere in the world. Had he read Grimm or the Arabian Nights, he might in some measure have been prepared for sights so wonderful, but he had never heard of fairy wands, or Aladdin lamps or invisible and omnipotent genii; and, therefore, not knowing how to account for such dazzling splendor, he stood astounded, with mouth agape. He was as busy differentiating his impressions as a child when the first rays of a dawning intelligence open its eyes to a world of variegated color and multiple form.

"Gawd!" he murmured under his breath, "she's way ahead of de train, and way past de whistle. What slum fer a crib-cracker!"*

On the sideboard was a large chocolate

*What booty for a safe or lock breaker.

cake which Master Garwood reached by the aid of a chair; he cut a large slice for himself, stepped down, and very generously invited the guest to take his turn.

The guest first nibbled at the cake to make sure it contained no poison, then smacking his lips he made haste to cut two slices, one of which he slipped into his pocket.

This last action shocked the good breeding of the prince. "My mamma says that ain't polite, to take two pieces."

The guest was not at all embarrassed, he was used to being caught in predicaments like that, and he coolly inquired what "perlite" might mean?

"It means — well, it means that you mus' n't take two pieces when company's here, or when they ain't."

"I guess yer mudder never eat no free lunch," ventured the Arab, his mouth so full of cake that he could scarcely speak.

"What's that?"

"Free lunch?   Dat 's grub what's thrung in wid de drinks."

The son thought his mother had never eaten of such food.

In the corner of the room on a mahogany table was a Chinese ivory carving, one of the first things that attracted the visitor's attention.

"What's dat Ching-Chang good fer?" he asked, pointing to the ivory.

"Oh, that? That's an ornament; you push its head, and it goes on shaking by itself — so."

The guest had never seen anything that struck his fancy more forcibly, and when the host was looking elsewhere he slipped it under his coat. But somehow he felt uncomfortable, he was taking unfair advantage of some one who had treated him kindly, and recognizing for the first time in his life that there was a line of demarcation between meum and tuum, he waited his opportunity and put the carving back. It had scarcely touched the table before the boy's mother made her appearance.

"Harvey, what are you doing with that cake? You know that you should n't touch it. I 've been looking all over the house for you, where have you been? Goodness me! Where did that child come from? Why did you bring him into the house? I shall never let you go out of the house again without the nurse.''

"The Kid'' pressed close to the wall, wishing with all his heart and soul that he could press clean through it into the street.

''He 's a fine boy,'' said Harvey in honest surprise, ''he can take things out of your pocket, and you can't see him do it; and he can sing funny songs and play drunk and spit way across the room.''

The queen paid no attention to the appeal of the little prince for his playmate, the pauper: ''If you do n't go at once, little boy, I must send you away.''

''Please, mum,'' he interposed, ''I did n't mean no harm; the kid tole me as you was good to de poor, and he tole me ter come in wid him. But you need n't fly de peeler, I 'll wing.''

''How glad I am that my dear child is n't a little vagabond like that,'' thought the mother, a few seconds after the boy had gone.

"Just de same," reflected "The Kid," on his way homeward, "I wish dat I had swiped de Ching-Chang wid de swingin' nut."

PART III.

HEREDITY—A POSSIBILITY.

"There's a boy in the reception room, that wants to see you. He says he has a very important message. Shall I admit him?"

"A boy with an important message for me, you say? Who is the boy, Mr. Runnels?"

From the slow, grave manner in which he spoke these few unimportant words you would have known that Mr. Garwood, Sr., a stern, yet withal benevolent appearing man of middle age, was precise and methodical in everything he did, whether the matter in hand involved pennies or thousands.

"I have n't the least idea, sir," answered the secretary, "but he looks like a very poor boy."

"I can't see him; I am very much pressed for time;" and he turned to read the correspondence that lay in neat, square piles on his desk.

"You might find out what he wants," he said as Mr. Runnels left the room.

"The boy will not go away, Mr. Garwood, nor will he tell me what he wants. He says the message is a matter of life and death, and he will deliver it only to you," said the secretary on returning.

"A matter of life and death," and the head of the great house of Garwood & Co. repeated the words in his characteristic, weighty manner. "Well, I presume it might be wise to see this important messenger from the fates." His curiosity was aroused, and he had calculated while speaking to Runnels that he could spare three minutes.

The door opened again, and a small boy, hat in hand, stepped across the Turkish rugs, and up to the millionaire's desk, as if he had crossed Turkish rugs every day of his life to interview millionaires in their private offices.

Mr. Garwood, toying with his whiskers,

eyed the boy from head to foot through his glasses. A few glances told him that the boy was fourteen or fifteen years of age, that he was poor to the extreme of want, and that he was a neat boy; for his clothes, worn as they were, looked as if excessive brushing and cleaning had worn the patches into them. He was an honest boy, for he looked one straight in the face with his large brown eyes, and did not flinch; he was an intelligent boy, too, for those eyes were mirrors of eagerness and vivacity.

The subject of this inspection interrupted any further conclusions with, "Are you Mr. Garwood?"

He nodded affirmatively, saying, "So you are the boy who has an important message for me, a message of life or death, I believe?"

"Yes," answered the lad, "so I has. I needs a job and I knows yer kin give me one." His voice and manner of speaking were so like Garwood Sr.'s that the latter might have imagined that he was being mocked. Had he not been prepossessed

in the boy's favor and amused by his manner, he would have ended the interview
then and there.

"So that is your message of life and
death, is it?" Mr. Garwood inquired, his
stern features relaxing into a good-natured
smile.

"It is fer me, sir, I kin tell yer; it's work
'er starve with me."

"H'm, and what can you do, if I should
offer you work?"

"Everything," was the ready response.

The plutocrat crossed his hands behind
his head and lolled back in his revolving
chair; he was going to allow himself a little
recreation at the boy's expense.

"It has been my experience that those
who boldly claim they can do everything,
in reality can do nothing."

"I spoke too quick, sir. I mean ter say,
I 'm willin' fer to do anything."

"You should never speak too quickly,
boy."

"Thank you, sir."

At the boy's "I thank you," the plutocrat's eye-glasses almost jumped away with a jerk from the silk cord to which they were attached. He thought he detected a ring of sarcasm in the voice, but the speaker's face remained grave as a deacon's.

"Well, and what value do you place upon your indispensable services?"

"My in-dis-pen-sa-ble services ought ter be worth four dollars a week," piped the urchin.

"Four dollars? When I started to work here at your age, they paid me but three, if I remember correctly."

"P'rhaps yer was n't worth no more," observed the applicant very quietly, as if quite sure of the truth of his remark.

The merchant's brows contracted into a scowl, then he burst out laughing and laughed until his sides ached. The boy laughed, too; he saw the humor of the situation and enjoyed it keenly. The former checked himself suddenly. "I have no more time to spend now. Return at three o'clock; I shall have more leisure then, and we shall see what can be done for you."

At three o'clock to the minute the boy put in his appearance.

"I am glad you 're so punctual,"remarked Mr. Garwood, "I 've been expecting you."

The vision of this naïve, cheerful waif, had the same invigorating effect on the overworked man of millions that a cool breeze wafted from the lake has upon the burning streets of the city.

"Yer know," began the boy, "I think yer an awful nice sort of a man."

"And what has given you that opinion of me?" Mr. Garwood was prepared for anything now.

"Well, Mrs. Steen tole me that a man what laughs right out from his inside that a way till his shoulders shake is allus honest, good-natered en kind-hearted, en what Mrs. Steen says yer kin bank on every time."

"Mrs. Steen, and who may that good lady be?"

"She 's the good woman what brung me up and saved my soul."

"Did n't you have a mother to do that for you?"

"Ef I had a mudder, she turned me out ter shift fer myself 'fore I had a chance ter know how handsome she was."

"You must have had a very hard struggle of it, my lad." This last was said sympathetically in a manner calculated to draw the boy out. He found himself more and more interested in this urchin who spoke to him with the nonchalance of a superior.

"Yer bet, I had a hard time of it. I most starved en froze ter death. Dern, if I know how I stood it long enuf fer Mike ter find me. There must be iron in me some'eres," he paused to reflect. Then, thinking that he was going to embark on a long story, he invited himself to be seated in the chair that stood in the corner at the right of the merchant's desk.

"I wish my boy had a little of this urchin's iron in his constitution, and less soft lead," thought Mr. Garwood, Sr.

"As I was saying," he went on with perfect equanimity, "I had tough times till I struck Mike, Mike's the bartender of The Lucky Number. Ever heard of The Lucky

Number? No? It's a joint where the hobos hangs out, and the toughs. Tough, gee whiz! those fellers is tough. They tried to make me tough es they was, en' they come near doin' it. They learned me ter swear, en smoke, en steal; none of 'em learned me no good, I kin tell yer.

"Mike took a shine ter me; he liked me 'cause I was smart en could swear back, en sass quicker 'en he could. He let me sleep there and onct in a while, just enuf to keep me livin', he fed me on free lunch. He liked me there, 'cause I amoosed the hobos by singin', drinkin', en playin' all around tough kid. I was tough, too, but I ain't proud of it now, dough I was den.

"En' I went on gettin' tougher en tougher till I runned into Mudder Steen; Mudder Steen is the woman what keeps the dressmakin' shop four blocks this side of The Lucky Number. I runned an errand fer her, after her girl went out ter take a dress, and could n't find the place of the woman what ordered it. I found it all right. After that she let me run all over the city fer her;

then she let me sleep in her shop, en give me my meals fer runnin' errands en keepin' the place clean.

"She was a Dutch woman, Mudder Steen, en stuck on goin' ter church; she made me go 'long ter church with her on Sundays, en go ter Sunday school. I did n't like it much at first en runned away, but she scared the life out of me tellin' about hell fire, en burnin'. She used ter cry 'cause I was so bad, en pray fer me, en tell me how it hurt her ter see me that a way. It hurt me, too, ter see the old woman cryin' en carryin' on, en I made up my mind all ef a sudden, en I quit bein' tough en bad from that day on. She used ter read ter me nights, en she learned me ter read, en write, en spell, en 'rithmetic. She knowed a heap, Mudder Steen did, even if her talk was Dutchy. One Christmas, 'cause I learned ter read so fast, she give me two books, Robinson Crusoe and 'Rabian Nights. I liked 'Rabian Nights best; 'specially 'bout the nigger that brought Aladdin the lamp and popped out of the ground whenever he rubbed it. It's a great story, yer ought ter read it.''

''I've read it,'' said the plutocrat seriously.

''And Friday and the —''

''I'm afraid you will have to draw your story of your life to a close, for I shall—''

''By the way,'' the boy with a history interrupted excitedly, ''how's your son, Harvey R. Garwood, Jr.? I meant ter ask en I forgot.''

''How in the wide world did you ever make the acquaintance of my son!'' ejaculated Garwood Sr.

''When I was only a kid, six years ago, I was going en errand fer Mike, en I lost my way, en I met him. We played together a long time, en talked, en he told me his pa was rich, en had a big factory, with large chimneys. He took me in his house, too, en we was havin' a good time till the old woman chased me out.''

''I have a dim recollection that my wife told me something of the kind some years ago.''

"I thought you'd remember if you heard it. Mudder Steen, when I tole her about it, used ter laugh, en she made me remember all about it, en keep tellin' her often so as not ter ferget. 'Ef ever anything happens ter me,' she says, 'you go ter see that Mr. Garwood en tell him jest what yer tellin' me, en he'll laugh en give yer the job.' Mudder Steen died last week, en the shop's gone, so I come."

"And you shall have the job, too, my lad, even if I prove your good Mother Steen wrong by not laughing. I shall have to get along with two office boys instead of one, I suppose."

"I don't want ter be no office boy, put me in the factory, I want ter learn a trade."

"I like your spirit, and in the factory you shall go, if the works have to be turned upside down to put you there."

When William Steen, for such was his name now, stepped down the long hallway leading to the factory, he said to the foreman who was leading him thither, "I'm going ter have yer job in ten years, watch out."

The foreman patted him on the head and laughed, but the very boldness of the remark captured his heart, and he resolved on the spot to do all in his power to advance the lad, even if he endangered his own position. And when he related this remark of the 'prentice to the factory hands they laughed still louder, if that were possible, but they admired the boy none the less for the courage he displayed in ''sassin' the boss.''

For a long time the remark passed current in the factory as a joke, and when they twitted him about it good-naturedly, as often happened, Will compressed his lips tightly and answered only, ''You'll see.'' And they did see.

''Watch out,'' the men would say to the foreman as the 'prentice passed on from stage to stage, from casting to turning, and from turning to fitting and burnishing, with a rapidity that astonished everybody. ''Watch out, or the kid, afore you know it, will push you out.''

Garwood Sr., who was watching the advance of his *protégé* with an interest akin to pride, never had cause to regret the day that he had given Will Steen a start in life. "I shall be satisfied," he said to his wife when Harvey left home for college, "if our son, with every advantage in his favor, succeeds as well at college as this Arab, whom I took from the streets, is succeeding in my factory."

The clink-clank of innumerable hammers on the anvils, the whistling of lathes, the whirl of great wheels, the activity and movement of the factory—all was music to Will's ear. His fondest dream anticipated the day when his command should send every man, like a soldier well drilled, to his post, and make the minutest part of the complicated machinery pulsate with the joy that comes from doing, creating.

In his heart was implanted a yearning for power, an eagerness to lead, to be at the head, and the higher he advanced in the factory the greater did this desire become. Instinctively, he felt that power comes from knowledge; and when the day's work was done he went to night-school, that he might gain the knowledge, which, by-and-by, he hoped, was to transform itself into power. His advance there was equally remarkable; he mastered books as readily as he made the iron, hot from the forge, take what shape he willed.

He was born to rule, and gifted as he was with foresight, policy and ability, he made things serve as a spring-board to bound him upward.

Before the expiration of ten years the foreman left for a more advantageous position, and Will Steen stepped into the place; his prophecy had been verified. He wasted no time resting on his oars; higher up the stream there were stations waiting for brain and executive ability, and it tantalized him to see the waters rush on while his boat stood still.

Clad in his overalls, he walked into the president's office one morning. "Mr. Garwood," said he, "I think that I can be of more service to you in the office than in the factory. Why not put me there to figure on your contracts?"

The president was somewhat skeptical, but he consented to give him a trial. Will Steen never asked for more than a trial; it was the start that always gave him the race.

The same persistent, tireless energy that he had put forth in factory and school won him the most responsible position in the office. He was fast nearing the end of the stream; he could catch the glimmer of the waters at the source, and he tugged at his oars with a violence which strained his muscles, that he might reach the goal before the current could carry him an inch downward.

In another five years he was Garwood Sr.'s right hand man with a small interest in the house of Garwood & Co. "I expected it," was all he said when the plutocrat called him to occupy a desk in his private office.

More than once did the millionaire repeat the wish that his own son might have some of Will Steen's iron in his flabby constitution, for Harvey R. Garwood Jr.'s vacillating will and idle life made the father despair for his future.

At nineteen he was expelled from his freshman year for drunkenness, gambling, and a neglect of his studies.

His parents were inconsolable. While their son's ability had never led them to believe that his career would be brilliant, they had hoped that his life might be at least honorable and free from all taint of dissipation. As a matter of course, there were the the tears of a penitent prodigal, the forgiveness of a trusting, confident mother, and of a firmer and more unrelenting father.

For a time his repentance seemed sincere, and when he started to work at his father's office he gave every promise of retrieving his lost reputation; but the promise proved a lie, for there followed a second period of reckless dissipation and evil associates. A second time the mother pleaded, the son promised, and the father forgave.

His third defection was more serious; Garwood Jr., for the purpose of meeting a debt contracted over the gambling table, forged Garwood Sr.'s name to a note. This time the mother pleaded and the son promised in vain, the father remained inexorable; he disowned his son and forbade that Harvey's name ever be mentioned in his presence.

Thus every time that Will Steen climbed up a round on the ladder of life, Harvey R. Garwood, Jr. slipped down two.

The erect tall frame of Garwood Sr. was slowly bending under the heavy burden of old age; his vitality was fast slipping from between his fingers, and he found Will's assistance and advice more and more necessary. A magnetic force — the irresistible force that draws like to like—drew Will to him closer and closer. The time came when he called Will and said, "You have been a son to me in all but name; you have taken a son's place in my office, come, take it in my home. My wife sent you away from there years ago as a vagabond; in her name, as well as in mine, I ask you to return as my son."

Not long after this epoch in his career Will entered the office with a face that clearly betokened a heavy heart. The older man with his quickness of perception noticed it instantly.

"Something has gone wrong, my boy, speak out. Is it something concerning Harvey? I am always expecting it. Have no secret from me; his past conduct has prepared me for the worst."

"I must say it sometime," replied Will, "and the sooner I say it, the sooner the thing is done; if I do n't break the news to you now, some one else will do it later and more abruptly. It is something terrible."

The old man nodded, looking the quintessence of will and self-control as he sat upright in his chair, holding its arms with his firm powerful hands.

"I read in this afternoon's paper that your son Harvey was shot last night at The Lucky Number!"

Aaron Pivansky's Picture

PART I.

THE PICTURE IS PAINTED.

IT was long past midnight when the idea that he had left his safe unlocked popped into the restless mind of Solomon Pivansky. Suspicions just as groundless had already wasted two of sleep's priceless hours, and being loathe to leave his warm bed he tried to argue this one to the same death that he had argued its fellows. But finding himself unable to effect a compromise between sleep and the idea, he arose grumblingly and made his way down the stairs which connected the sleeping apartment with the pawn-shop.

You can imagine his astonishment at finding the lamp burning at full height in the rear room of the pawn-shop; but you cannot imagine his astonishment at finding his son Aaron leisurely giving the finishing touches to a large canvas stretched across an artist's easel. Astonishment is not the word; Solomon was dumbfounded, so dumbfounded that his vocabulary, giving his tongue the slip, left him without the means of expressing his surprise in a full half-dozen of those racy epithets in which Yiddish abounds. The sight of all this artist's paraphernalia formed an instantaneous association in Solomon's mind with the figure of the penniless artist Brosseau, who had been obliged to pawn "the stuff" in order to eke out another day's miserable existence. Solomon did not intend that his son's soul should thrive at the expense of his body, and he gave the easel a kick that sent the canvas on the floor with a bang, and his hand struck out simultaneously for Aaron's face. The blow never reached home, however, for the boy caught his father's outstretched hand by the wrist and held it firmly. This was the first time in his life that any of the Pivanskys had dared to dispute his parental authority, and Solomon's blood rose to the boiling point.

His face was mean enough ordinarily, literally, as well as figuratively, without a redeeming feature,—a harsh, hard, cunning, repulsive face, a face that made it useless for the owner to deny sordidness and avarice and tyranny, a face that bore the marks and showed the results of thirty years of Russian persecution, and a face that bespoke a sullen waiting for the hour of vengeance. Mean enough ordinarily, I said, but you should have seen it then, when anger accentuated its brutal inhumanity.

A wrench, and he freed his arm from Aaron's grasp. " I 'll show you," he muttered, "before the night's over who 's master here. So this is the way you waste my oil and my time, is it? I never can get any work out of you. No wonder you fall asleep over your work, and leave the stock and the books to keep themselves. I 'll show you! Is it for this that I let you go two years to school, and waste

my hard-earned money, you good-for-noth-
ing!''

At every word of the diatribe Solomon's
face grew darker, that part at least, which
was not covered by his black, frowzy beard.
Aaron knew what to expect and he waited
calmly, standing squarely in front of his canvas that had fallen back-foremost, resolved
whatever befell him to protect it from injury.

Pivansky, the elder, foresaw his intention.
''I'll smash that thing to pieces when I get
through with you.''

''No, you'll not,'' retorted Aaron, assum-
ing an offensive position.

Had Solomon seen a lamb changed to a
lion before his eyes, the miracle would not
have astounded him so much as this sudden
change from fearful obedience to defiant
disobedience on the part of his Aaron, usually as meek as Moses, and he stood dum-
founded again.

War had been declared, and Aaron meant
to push things to an issue, then and there.
''I have spent a year on that picture; I have

toiled nights on it after the day's hard labor, while you and other men slept; if you ruin it you might as well kill me and be done with it; for I can never gather the courage to attempt a work like that again, and I would rather die than waste my life in this nasty pawn-shop.   I 'm sick of it, and I 'm above it.''

"Above it, are you?" shouted Solomon— "above it?   Well, I'll bring your stiff neck down to it, quick enough.''

It would have gone hard with the young artist had not Mrs. Pivansky (a short, fat woman, with nothing to distinguish her from the other thousand and one women of the Ghetto) made her appearance at this juncture of affairs and delayed the unequal combat.   She had been awakened by the noise, and, astonished not to find her husband at her side, had rushed down stairs to find out the cause of the disturbance.

"A nice son you 've raised,'' said her husband, turning towards her; "he 's a *gonef* *; he stole this stuff from the shop, and he's

*A thief.

stealing my time to paint his trashy pictures.''

She stood in open-mouthed stupidity, trying to make head and tail out of this unexpected jumble.

"If he paid attention to the business he might amount to something. Let him buy something with his pictures." He thundered this last observation at his wife, as if she were to blame for her son's lack of commercial astuteness.

"Yes," she answered stupidly, "let him buy something with his pictures."

Aaron knew the weakness of his parents, and with true Jewish perspicacity he bent the trend of the argument to his own advantage. "Buy something with that picture! I can sell it for more than your pawn-shop is worth. It will make me rich and famous— it's a work of art. An artist with years of training and every opportunity of study would be proud to have painted it." His tone was at once persuasive and conciliatory. "It will make us rich, that picture," he spoke as one who speaks from one's soul-belief.

Money! The word acted like the touch of a talisman, it made the whole affair appear different in Solomon's eyes; he had never thought of the possibility of converting paint to gold. He reflected for a second or two, trying to calculate what the picture might be worth. "Let's see the thing," he snapped.

Proudly Aaron lifted the picture from the floor, and held it up to the light. For over a year he had yearned for an opportunity to show his father what he had done, but he had always been restrained by the fear that his effort would displease him, and that his displeasure would assume some such violent semblance as it had worn on this night.

Wonderful and strange difference between the father and son. I might contrast their characters and their appearances for pages and pages, and then have left untouched those finer shades and subtler shadows which are not seen at the first, nor yet at the second or third glance.

Aaron had the countenance of a man who aspires; a soulful, yearning face, one that would willingly gaze forever on the stars above, but which circumstance forces to look on the earth below. The long battle fought between pawn-shop and art-studio for the possession of Aaron's soul had moulded every line of its contour; and the dumb appeal of the heart, which helplessly watched the superior brutal force of the pawn-shop strive to dominate the spiritual force of the art-studio, had somehow found expression in the beseeching glances of two dark eyes, made pathetic by the constant reflection of such intense heart-suffering. The battle was still waging persistently, and needed but the force of shifting circumstances to throw its balance of power one way or the other and decide the victory.

Solomon's mortification at his son's performance rapidly gave way to an emotion of pleasure at the first glance at the picture, and mauger his best efforts to appear indifferent, he could not hide his interest and admiration. And his wife Rachel, usually impassive and indifferent, the impassiveness and indifference of sheer stupidity, burst forth into exclamations of surprise and wonder as she looked from the artist to the picture, and from the picture to the artist, as if trying to unfathom the mystery of their correlation.

Aaron's anger at his father's harshness was carried away by an overwhelming tidal wave of the pride and joy of first success; and after the fashion of all tyros in art, he was arguing that since his picture had made an impression on the flinty heart of the father, and the obtuse sensibilities of the mother, it could not fail to impress the world at large, and bring him in one bound to fame and fortune.

Small wonder that the boy's masterpiece interested those two, since he had taken their most familiar religious rite, surrounded it with the unfamiliar, and by the magic of his art made visible an inherent sublimity and pathos they had never known it to possess. The familiar interested; the unfamiliar, child of the painter's fancy, won their admiration and awakened their awe.

The picture represented the observance of *Yom Kippur* on the battlefield of Metz by the Jewish section of the German army. The center of the canvas was occupied by a *chasan,** who loomed forth in majestic proportions as he rested on the altar and lifted his voice in the sacred song of the *Kol Niedre;* but to his shoulders clung not the harsh covering of the uniform of war, but the soft folds of the *talith,* emblem of religious worship. Behind the altar (evidently a temporary affair, constructed in haste), mountain and forest and valley stretched away in the interminable sweep of perspective. The darkness of the falling night was broken by the light that came from the candles burning at the *chasan's* side, and from the flame of the "eternal lamp" which hung suspended over his head. The coigns of vantage were held by huge burnished cannon, stationed there to guard the worshippers from a sudden attack of the enemy. In the foreground were assembled curious groups of German soldiery, who

*A chanter.

looked on these mystic exercises with an air of commingled pity and contempt.

I must leave the reader's imagination to fill in the bare outline given, with the dread instruments and imagery of war, the sublimity and pomp of religious ceremony, and the calmness of exterior nature breathing peace and good will to man. Touching epitome of the sad history of Israel's weary sojourn among the nations, this picture of Aaron Pivansky's; with what infinite pathos did he bespeak the fateful separation of his people from the peoples of the earth,—with them always, but of them, alas, how rarely.

In the flotsam and jetsam of the pawn-shop the boy had found a history of the Franco-Prussian war, and in that history (read with avidity, one may be sure) he found a few lines touching upon the incident just described, and, Doré-like, he had taken those few lines and made them teem with the passing fancies and conceptions and visions of his dreams.

His perspectives were by no means true, his color values often false, and his drawing lacked the certainty that comes of much practice; but in spite of these major defects and numerous minor ones, it was a creation of which a boy of twenty might well be proud. All he knew of the technique of his art had been taught him by one Brosseau, an habitué of L'Auberge, who painted that he might drink, and drank that he might paint; so one knew not whether to blame his art for keeping him a drunkard, or liquor for keeping him an artist. When he could not sell his pictures to a saloon he pledged them at a pawn-shop; he had a local reputation at least, this Brosseau — saloonkeepers and pawnbrokers knew he was an artist.

Aaron heard of him, cultivated his acquaintance, and spent every minute that he could steal from the shop in Brosseau's company. Brosseau taught him all he knew, because he loved the boy for the good that was in him, and for the yearning and the aspiration that had once been his own; and with Aaron he left the gutters to enter again the divine temple of art.

Besides Brosseau he found one other

source of instruction, the Art Gallery; here he spent the longed-for, prayed-for Saturday afternoons when the pawn-shop was closed, and when to Aaron it seemed that art and leisure, twin sisters with arms ever intertwined, swayed the universe, and did not deny the inspiration of their presence even to the somber narrow streets of the Ghetto.

His work was done mostly in the small hours of the night, long after the family had retired, and when he himself was worn out by the tedium of his daily task. Often did he toil until the breaking of dawn warned him of the coming of the day, then he hid his canvas carefully, and crawled to bed for a few hours of restless slumber, dream-disturbed. Surely, surely in hours like these when, despite his heroic will, he fell asleep over his work, the angel of beautiful dreams, who visited Fra Angelico, Raphael and Luca della Robbia, could not resist the temptation to whisper the secret of the mystery of things in this boy's ear, and to entwine about his brow an invisible wreath, woven of inspiration, and fame, and promise, and the message of God.

Solomon looked up from the picture with a yawn. "You painted the *Omed** too high," was his only comment. "Go to bed, you," he said, turning towards his wife and son. Rachel followed the instructions without argument or expostulation, as was her wont.

"What are you going to do with the picture?" queried Aaron.

"Nothing," snarled Solomon. "Go to bed."

In the morning he found his masterpiece in the show window, where space for it had been cleared, and already, early as the hour was, a group of curious people had been attracted by the work, and were lavishing praise upon it that knew neither measure nor bound.

"Even if my father says nothing," thought Aaron, "he is proud of me, and he wants people to know that he has a son who can do a work like that." And he went

*The Altar.

about his distasteful tasks as if his heart were in them, that he might show the father his kindness did not go unheeded and unappreciated.

PART II.

THE PICTURE IS SOLD.

No one in the Ghetto save Becky Cohen suspected that Solomon Pivansky's son nourished any thought that rose above the debit and credit line of his father's ledger; but she was as Aaron's left hand, knowing whatever his right hand did. Becky's mother kept the combination book-shop and bakery, which gave the girl a two-fold opportunity — often lacking, alas! — of caring for mind and body equally, so one never went hungry that the other might fatten.

Becky had devoured all the books in her mother's shop, some fifty and odd, with even a greater eagerness than she devoured the "*kicklach*,"* and she showed her partiality for the books by devouring them over

*Cakes.

and over again. They were all romances of high life, seen through the wrong end of an opera-glass, and made to seem very high indeed; so high, that Becky's eyes were strained from constantly looking upward, and she found herself unable to look down to where life had placed her.

While her hands were busy waiting on customers, her mind was wandering afar, holding imaginary conversations with dukes and duchesses.

She, like Aaron, had been gifted with imagination, but unfortunately it had been twisted in the wrong direction, and was productive of nothing better than empty and idle dreams; while his, mastered by a firm will and a healthy ambition, was creative and powerful.

Becky, thus nourished on romance and pastry, grew rapidly to her teens, and became a healthy and comely maid to look upon, a little too stout, perhaps, but comely for all of that, with features regularly cast in a Jewish mould, with black hair, and sloe-black eyes that under two heavy long

lashes danced merrily, and a complexion—
this is the finishing stroke of the photograph
—that was by contrast strikingly fair and
ruddy, and made two rows of perfect teeth
show to rare advantage whenever she opened
her pretty mouth to laugh, which, you may
be sure, was very often.

It was their very longing in common for
higher things, this ambition to be something
above what they were, that drew Becky and
Aaron together and made them fast friends.
Often, weary and sick of battling against
such odds, he might have given up the
struggle had not her words of consolation
and encouragement intervened and armed
him with new resolution.

She went to the Art Gallery with him,
and always managed to bring their visits to
an end in front of one of Millet's pictures.
"See," she would say, "what this man
did, and you, yourself, have often told me he
had fewer advantages than you, and far
more to contend against." Then Aaron
would answer nothing, but would compress
his lips tightly and resolve in his heart to

become a great painter like Millet, and never to give up trying until death.

Had it not been for Becky, the young aspirant would have left his home and taken desperate chances against starvation for the love of his art, but she pointed out the folly of such a course, and forced him to bide his time impatiently. Her one hope for a position in the greater world was Aaron, and she did not propose to allow that hope to commit involuntary suicide. In the odd mixture of qualities that went to make up Becky, one large grain of common sense had luckily found its way, and given taste and flavor to the whole.

When he told her of his last great inspiration, and how he feared that he had neither the skill nor the training necessary to work out so sublime a subject, and save it from being ridiculous; she, seeing at a glance, the vast possibilities it contained, urged him on, now by a word of encouragement, now by a word of praise, and, when all these failed, by whole sentences of scorn. The work once fairly under way, she kept his ambition

at fever heat, and never allowed him to lag
or grow despondent.   If the artist feared
the work was not progressing fast enough,
she proved to him that it was progressing
too fast; and if he feared that the work was
progressing too fast, she proved with equal
facility that it did not progress fast enough.

She was one of the first to spy the picture
in the window; and, after finding out from
the artist how this came about, she silently
took her place in the increasing crowd, and
llistened eagerly to all comments; and whenever anything of importance was said, she
stored the words away in her memory that
she might have the pleasure of repeating
them to Aaron verbatim.

The next evening as Aaron was slowly
returning homeward after the execution of
an errand in the neighborhood, his hands
thrust in his pockets, his head knocking
against the stars, and a Jewish melody on
his lips, he heard Becky calling, and he
stayed his steps to await her coming.

She was pale, breathless, visibly perturbed and anxious; he saw at a glance

that something had gone wrong, and he felt intuitively that it concerned his picture.

"Becky, what's the matter?" he asked.

"O Aaron, your picture"—the words seemed to stick in her throat as if of too dire portent to be spoken at once.

"Come, out with it; I know it's something bad; I'm ready to hear it."

She covered her face with her hands, afraid to look at him, as if she had been responsible for the misfortune. "Your father sold it," she cried out, rather than spoke.

"I'll get it back, mark that," he called, darting down the street. As he ran past the shop he glanced at the window in the hopeless hope of finding his picture still there.

Solomon stood behind the counter busily assorting an oblong tray of rings. On seeing him, he looked up and said in an unusually good-natured way, "I sold your picture for you."

The words and manner of saying them quite disarmed Aaron, and he stood unable to hurl one of the thousand invectives that shot barbed and pointed to his lips. In the short run from Becky to the shop, his nimble wit, distancing his feet, had preconceived his father's line of defense, and had laid in accordance therewith a plan of counter-attack; but the enemy used unwonted tactics, and he found his preparations mere impedimenta.

"Sold it, sold it for me; you talk as if you really believed that you had done me a favor," shrieked Aaron, his face white with rage, and his small thin body quivering with excitement.

"There are fools and fools," remarked Solomon with a sententious shrug of the shoulders. "Can you get twenty dollars for *mashofes** like that every day?"

"Twenty dollars!" Such paltry pay for a deed so base, so despicable. His heart clung to his ribs to keep from sinking; his breast heaved and fell as though it would burst asunder; and the tears trickled down his throat, rather than swept to his eyes;

*Trash.

some seconds passed before he could trust
himself to speak.

"Twenty dollars! Do you mean to say
you were fool enough to sell it for twenty
miserable dollars? Were you out of your
mind when you sold it? Who bought it,
who? Speak quick, there may be time to
get it back. I'll buy it back again for
eighty."

He grasped the door knob, ready to start
on hearing the name of the purchaser. The
picture, once recovered, he meant that his
father should hear more from him concerning this night's transaction, but now time was
precious, too precious to waste in futile quar-
rel and recrimination.

Solomon's self assurance left him, and he
was thoroughly crestfallen; for once in his
life he feared that he had driven a bad bargain. The boy was right, he was a fool, he
should have held out longer; without
further solicitation he described the purchaser to the best of his ability, but who he
was and where he lived, Solomon did not
know.

"I'll come back when I find my picture and not until then; if I don't find it, you'll never see me here again," and with these words firmly and resolutely spoken, Aaron slammed the door and was gone.

"When he's hungry enough he'll come back, and that won't be long," said Solomon to his wife an hour later, as he related to her what had happened.

But all that night she sat up waiting for the sound of his knock at the door, and many another weary night did she sit waiting and longing with a "*Bornch Habo*"* on her lips. But he did not come to end the agonizing tedium of her vigils, or to give the only reward she asked in return for her love, her sacrifice, and forbearance—the sound of his knock at the door.

*Blessed be he who cometh.

PART III.

THE PICTURE IS FOUND.

Aaron brought all the wit, all the wisdom and all the energy that were his into active play in the search for his picture; but the play was one of pure chance, skill counted for naught. So the weeks sped on and left him without even as much as a clue to its whereabouts.

The opportunity to express himself in his art had been his all-in-all, subtract it from the sum of things that made his world and the result was a zero. Now that it seemed farther off and more unattainable than ever, he grew despondent, misanthropic, his strength of character proving his weakness and dragging him downward with the same force by which it had guided his flight upward.

On one gloomy, rainy day, it chanced that Aaron, more atrabilious than the weather, found himself in the neighborhood of the Art Gallery, and deluded with the idea

that it was for the sake of the shelter, and
not to gratify the desire of seeing again the
paintings of his beloved masters (he affected
to believe that his love for all that concerned his craft had turned into aversion),
he went thither.

Near the entrance on the main floor, was a
large placard announcing the fact that the
pictures competing for the "S—scholarship"
were hung in the ante-room to the left of
the stairway. This "S—scholarship," offered
annually by a multi-millionaire, entitled the
winner to a two-year residence for study at
Paris. Aaron knew of this prize; but he had
made the resolve to wait another year or
two, and then — go to Paris.

In the anger and rabid jealousy of his
mood, a mood that was fast centering and
fashioning itself into a temperament, he
resolved "to cut" the ante-room, and deny
it the honor of his presence. What interest
was there for him in this battle of the pictures, since he was denied the right to wield
a brush? He passed the room some three or
four times, and then condescended to enter

that he might pass an adverse criticism which was to include the whole collection in one prejudiced sweep. The first canvas his eye happened to fall upon, the one occupying the most conspicuous place in the exhibition, was his own.

Have you ever seen the reflection of your image in a glass at the end of a long corridor, and been bewildered for an instant by the strong resemblance the approaching,— and shall I say august, — personage bears to yourself? A second, and the illusion is broken, and you stand blandly smiling at the mistake. In the infinitesimal division of a minute that separated the discernment from the absolute recognition of his picture, Aaron experienced a similar sensation. The idea struck him forcibly that he had seen that subject, or one much like it, on canvas before; then it dawned upon him, like a flash, that the picture was his.

He wasted no time in threading the labyrinth through which it must have passed before reaching this destination, but forthwith he sought the director of the Institute, and poured into his ears the story of the picture and all his woes.

He was so perturbed and excited that he wandered in his narrative, spoke inconsequentially, repeated the same facts in a slightly different way, and appeared to contradict himself; his age, too, gainsaid the probability of his boasted accomplishments, and the director failed to be convinced.

"Even if wrong had been done you," he said, "it would be beyond my power to right it. However, you might see the president of the Institute," and he wrote the name and address for him.

To speak in contumelious phrase the scorn and hatred he felt for the man, was Aaron's first impulse; but he restrained himself, not wishing to snatch away the last straw from his drowning hope.

When he finally found the president, that dignitary treated his story with greater incredulity than the director, and suggested that he might see another official.

Thus after being sent from pillar to post, and from post to pillar, Aaron returned to the Art Gallery, sore of foot and heavy of heart, desperate, and willing to set sail with any wind, to risk his craft on any sea.

Since they had denied him justice, he would administer it with his own hands. He thrust his opened jack-knife into his pocket, walked up the stairs, sought the room where his work hung, and squarely in front of it he took his stand.

Woe to the dastardly sycophant of the brush if he found him there! He desired that the thief should be present, and should discover himself by some action or word regarding this *chef d'œuvre* and then—! But, fortunately for Aaron, this time, his desire was frustrated; scores of people commented on the achievement, had this to say in blame, and this to say in praise, and then passed on to exercise their critical faculties on some other canvas.

Not a word was said that could warrant Aaron's suspicion, crouching in the air, as it were, and eager to spring, in fastening on the speaker. If the thief were there, he sedulously avoided the locality where his putative *chef d' œuvre* hung.

The oddity of the subject, the boldness and vividness of treatment drew the crowd to Aaron's creation, and it was crowned the popular favorite. From the "wonderfuls, grands, masterlys" that streamed steadily from these gushing fonts of art criticism, he concluded that his picture was easily in the lead, and could not fail to win the prize; nor did he need the *vox populi* to make him believe the choice the *vox Dei*. By his own independent judgment he arrived at this modest conclusion, and, immodest as his conclusion may have been, it certainly rested upon firmer ground than a quicksand of conceit.

The praise he found too unctuous; instead of appeasing his anger it made him fairly quiver in vexation of spirit. So somebody else was to go to Paris on the ticket that his brain had won; somebody else to gain an education by the work of his hand! And must he sit quietly with arms folded and submit to robbery and injury without even lifting his voice in protest? He would see.

Towards noon the room emptied; the crowd drifting away, one by one, left Aaron alone with his anger.   He stepped into the hall; it was likewise deserted; up the broad marble-stairs no one was ascending.   He glided back to his masterpiece; and lifted his knife, ready to deface it beyond recognition. Every muscle and nerve of his body contracted so tensely and pulled inward and downward with such force that he felt dizzy as one suffering from a vertigo, and he almost lost his balance.

"How can I?" he thought, and feeling like a mother who has lifted a weapon to slaughter her babe, he let the knife fall at his side.   Breathing heavily, his heart beating against his ribs with ponderous, triphammer strokes, he half shut his eyes, and plunged the blade into the heart of the praying *chasan*.   He had breathed such life and vitality into this central figure, he had drawn its every line with such sympathy and feeling, he had watched it take form with

such reverence and love, that for him it was no mere semblance, but something vital and breathing; small wonder, hence, that he heard a mournful groan when the steel pierced the *chasan's* heart; small wonder, hence, that he heard a murmur of horror arising from the worshippers at this sacrilegious deed!

When the canvas was slashed into shreds, he stood aghast at what he had done, and then, biting his lip to suppress the sob that was rending his bosom, he hastened down the stairs and into the street.

**

While Aaron had been employing every faculty in the search for his picture, Becky was equally preoccupied in her search for Aaron. Moreover, she used his methods, looking in the likely places first, in the unlikely ones next, and then starting all over again.

Time and time again she had gone to the Art Gallery expecting to find him there; but she had always returned a link nearer the end of the chain of expectation to which she was clinging so tenaciously.

She did not grow gloomy or despondent, however (gloom and despondency never take root in a soil so unfavorable), for deep down in her heart was the faith, strong as conviction, that somehow, somewhere, Aaron and she would meet again, that they must meet. It always happened that way in the novels, and her romance was of the stuff from which novels are spun,—such novels, of course, as she read;—and if it didn't end that way in this specific case, she intended thereafter to read up to the last chapter only, and then stop, "for the rest is lies."

Every day found her at Mrs. Pivansky's with a beam of sunshine to brighten the darkness of the poor woman's life. What if the rays were fictitious; what if she did have to concoct little stories about having seen Aaron here or there, or that he was sure to find his picture on the morrow, "blessed to-morrow," and that he would surely be home the day after; what matters it whether such faery beams were factitious, as long as they brought light and cheer to a breaking heart?

She had always closed her mother's shop
at nine o'clock, but now she kept it open a
full hour longer, fondly cherishing the faith,
dying one minute, resuscitated the next, that
before the end of another sixty seconds she
might hear the low whistle, three-noted, that
had always signalled the hour of their tryst.

More than once, in passing her shop, had
Aaron caught a glimpse of Becky as she sat
on a low stool behind the counter, reading
her novels. And more than once did he
have to struggle vigorously against the
temptation to call her, that he might gain
the comfort and cheer she alone could give,
and for which he yearned; but the temptation was always mastered by an empty pride
and haughtiness of mood that forbade him
to see her until his picture be found.

Just as Becky closed her shop on the
night of that same day on which Aaron had
destroyed his treasure paramount, she heard
his familiar whistle. "It 's Aaron, it must be
Aaron!" she cried, running to open the
door.

She had often coined a speech, tender and

soulful, to say to him whenever favoring fortune should bring them together; now she found herself face to face with him, unable to voice even a commonplace.

She extended her hand and he, clasping it, remained silent; both felt as if the sands of an hour glass were running over their palms. What thoughts and sentiments arose from the darkness of a brain confused, and came to life at the clasp of those hands!

Aaron was the first to break that voluble silence. "I came to bid you good-bye, Becky; I am going away, perhaps forever," he said falteringly. "Brosseau has some decorating work to do out of town, and he is going to take me with him; we go to-night."

"Going away to-night and you come to tell me of it only now? Your neglect has been shameful, Aaron; more than that, you have been cruel, for you must have known how I suffered from your absence; and you knew, too, what change a word from you would have made in my life."

Over the boy's face, wan and peaked as

an invalid's, there passed an expression so
tristful, so pathetic in its appeal for sympathy that Becky felt the sharpness of the
rebuke turn inward, like a thrust from a
two-edged sword, and cut her to the quick;
and seeing with womanly intuition how
much her hero must have suffered since she
had met him last, her heart went out to
him in his suffering.

"Becky," he said, "you blame me too
severely, more than I deserve. I 've longed
to see you, I fairly ached to speak to you
again. More than once I started to come
here to let you know how I was getting
along, but things went so badly with me
that I could n't, I was ashamed to come.
It may have been false pride, it may have
been foolishness; call it what you like, but I
could n't overcome it."

Then with a fire and fervor that would
have melted slag, much more a tender heart
like Becky's, he told her how the quest for
his picture had ended.

"And now," he concluded, I must go
at once, I can't delay; I have good reason

for thinking that the police are hunting for me, and if they catch me they will surely send me to jail. And what wrong have I done? The picture was mine, I painted it, and if I destroyed it, I wronged myself and no one else.''

Of his dreams, his striving and endeavors this was the end; for having attempted to reach the ideal, he was condemned to skulk in gutters like an outlaw. Icarius-like, he had tried to reach the heavens, but the rough storms of circumstance had crippled his rare Dædalian wings, too weak for flight so high, and he fluttered moaning, helpless to the ground.

When he had finished Becky tried to give utterance to the sorrow and disappointment she felt, but her feeling was too surcharged with emotion to permit of translation into words; and born down by the weight of it, she fell weeping and sobbing into his arms.

''Do you understand why I must go? Do you forgive me for going?'' he asked, holding her tenderly.

''It 's not for you, Aaron, to ask forgiveness, but for me," answered Becky, contritely, regaining her self-possession, "and you may be assured that the others who have wronged you will ask it, too, before long. Don't go away, Aaron; stay here and fight for your rights to the bitter end; your very staying here is a proof of your innocence. If you go away, you know what they will say; you know how they will sneer."

"I have made up my mind to go, and nothing can change my decision. I hate this place; every step I take reminds me of my failure. And if the worst comes to the worst, and they take me and send me to jail, what then? I would rather die than stand the disgrace of it. No, I *must* go."

Then, smiling through her tears, Becky answered in those noble words that time, unwilling to let die, caught and turned into everlasting pearls as they fell from the lips of Ruth: "Whither thou goest, I will go, and where thou diest, will I die, and there will I be buried: the Lord do so to me, and more also, if aught but death part me and thee."